A Candlelight
Ecstasy Romance®

"NO MAN WILL EVER OWN ME!" SHANDA CRIED.

"But you are mine." York pulled her close to him. "You were meant to be mine."

"No!" Shanda struggled to break free. "You mean to capture my spirit but I am a Gypsy in my soul. Your world is not mine. You have me imprisoned in your chains of love."

He moved to quiet her struggling. "Can't you see how you enchant me, Shanda? When you look into the future, my beautiful Gypsy, do you see that I'm a cad who means to harm you?"

"I can see that you and I have no future at all," she whispered. But she knew this was a lie. He had stolen her heart and her Gypsy soul—he had bound her to him forever.

CANDLELIGHT ECSTASY ROMANCES®

GYPSY RENEGADE

Megan Lane

A Candlelight Ecstasy Romance®

Published by
Dell Publishing Co., Inc.
1 Dag Hammarskjold Plaza
New York, New York 10017

Dell ® TM 681510, Dell Publishing Co., Inc.

Candlelight Ecstasy Romance®, 1,203,540, is a registered
trademark of Dell Publishing Co., Inc., New York, New York.

ISBN: 0-440-13280-0

Printed in the United States of America

April 1986

10 9 8 7 6 5 4 3 2 1

WFH

To Lydia, Maggie, and Emily, for their unfailing encouragement and enthusiasm —with thanks.
For my husband, Robert, my sister, Ellen, and my dear friend Kathy—always.
And for everyone everywhere who has a little bit of the Gypsy in his or her soul.

To Our Readers:

We have been delighted with your enthusiastic response to Candlelight Ecstasy Romances®, and we thank you for the interest you have shown in this exciting series.

In the upcoming months, we will continue to present the distinctive, sensuous love stories you have come to expect only from Ecstasy. We look forward to bringing you many more books from your favorite authors and also the very finest work from new authors of contemporary romantic fiction.

As always, we are striving to present the unique, absorbing love stories that you enjoy most—books that are more than ordinary romance. Your suggestions and comments are always welcome. Please write to us at the address below.

Sincerely,

The Editors
Candlelight Romances
1 Dag Hammarskjold Plaza
New York, New York 10017

Dance, Gypsy woman,
By the firelight bright,
Dance, Gypsy woman,
Deep into the night.

Dance, Gypsy woman,
While the violins play,
Dance, Gypsy woman,
Steal his heart away.

CHAPTER ONE

The Gypsy music coaxed and cried, the harmony of violin and guitar casting a magical spell over the elite New York audience while Shanda Nicholas waited in the wings to make her entrance. The young male musicians picked up the beat, causing the feverish notes to fling themselves wildly into the enchanted watching faces.

The lights dimmed; a single stream of gold barely illuminated the handsome features of the Gypsy men as it focused on a black side curtain where Shanda suddenly burst onto center stage with a single fantastic leap.

She paused in a spellbinding pose, as if she were a beautiful figment of the audience's imagination, letting them watch her while she covertly studied them, her jade eyes hidden behind the fan of her fingers.

The music slowed; the melody became a passionately haunting strain. Provocatively, Shanda edged her long fingers aside to reveal a dramatic face with huge green eyes fringed by long black lashes, a slim, aristocratic nose, and voluptuous lips outlined in darkest glossy red.

She let her hands cup her heart-shaped face and trace the long, lithe shape of her upper body while she moved sinuously, her light olive skin the rich color of honey under the golden light spilling down on her. Her flaming red dress molded to her high firm breasts and tiny waist, hugged her hips, then flared out into many layers of multicolored material which descended to the floor.

She closed her eyes, her lovely profile revealing huge gold hoop earrings and black hair drawn into a severe chignon. Slowly, sensuously, she arched her neck, circled patterns in the air with her arms and began to snap her fingers, making the audience hold its breath in anticipation.

As Shanda began to tap her heel in a rhythmic *zapateado* beat, she looked at her audience. She could see from beneath her thick, lowered lashes that she had the sophisticated New Yorkers in the palm of her hand, especially one man sitting at a table directly in front of center stage.

She smiled at him to make the contact more immediate, and when she opened her eyes wide to capture him in her green gaze, she realized that he was staring at her.

Discreetly sizing him up, Shanda noted the careless way he wore his straight black hair, the spark in his dark eyes, and the reckless way he dressed, so casual in contrast to the suits of most of the other men.

14

A slow smile played on his lips, and one brow arched up in amusement as Shanda continued to look at him, drawing him into her world of snapping fingers, tapping heels, and Gypsy music. They seemed to be locked in some timeless moment, but abruptly the music changed and she whirled away from him with a feeling of relief.

Her dance, as unique as the woman herself, was part Gypsy-flamenco and all pure Shanda. She had been born to a legacy of music and dance, and rhythm was as natural to her as the air she breathed —and as necessary. As she moved across the stage to the glittering notes of the Gypsy song, she could say with her body what it would take another woman a thousand words.

Oddly, the man's face lingered in her mind, even when she shut her eyes against it. Her whirling dance drew her back before him again, and she opened her dark green eyes and looked once more into his. He has Gypsy eyes, she thought, but he was no Gypsy. He was a *gajó*—an outsider. All non-Gypsies were outsiders, and as such, taboo.

The music changed again, and Shanda changed with it, coming fully alive with the bold beat, letting it wash through her body and brain until she no longer saw the audience, not even the *gajó* who had unexpectedly heated her Romany blood for a single foolish moment.

Lifting her full skirt and petticoats high, she used the gifts of her Gypsy blood to reveal the fire ever burning in her soul. Like a moth to a flame, Shanda was lured to the *gajó* who sat so near the stage. As she

15

watched, he leaned over and whispered something to his blond companion.

"A man could get burned by that much fire," York Summerfield murmured to his longtime friend Hellyn Anderson.

"And you'd like to see how badly," Hellyn quipped.

"Damned right," York admitted. "She's magnificent."

They both laughed, and York turned back to the dancer.

Shanda suspected that he had been talking about her, and her temper flared at the thought of the laughter that had followed. Angry for speculating about such an unimportant matter, and angry for caring what he might say, she gave the dark-eyed stranger a false smile, then turned her back to him and let the beat of the music and the motion of her own body drum him from her head.

"She's as beautiful from the back as the front," York murmured, more to himself than to Hellyn as he noted the arched curve of the dancer's spine and the beauty of her long neck.

"I think she likes you," Hellyn said.

York was pensive for a moment, then he laughed again. "She probably didn't even really notice me. She's an entertainer, and obviously quite skilled in wooing her audience."

"She noticed," Hellyn drawled wryly. "Most women do. That's your problem. You're too spoiled. No man should have the easy access to the most beautiful women in the world that you have."

She shook her head as she let her blue eyes rove

16

over his straight black hair, big dark brown eyes, and finely chiseled jaw. "Especially no man as attractive as you. You're a menace, York. A thirty-year-old menace. I'm glad I never attracted more than your friendship."

He laughed again. "Lighten up, Hellyn. I only dress the models. I don't seduce them all."

"Only because you have so little time, and you know it. Being fashion designing's darling of the year takes more time than you'd like to give to it. You have other pursuits that interest you more."

He laughed. "Life is too short not to make the most of every beautiful moment," he retorted with a winning smile as he continued to stare at the Gypsy beauty.

She might not have really looked at him, but he had given careful attention to her every detail. She was the most exquisite creature he had ever seen, more enchanting than any of the models he chose from all over the world to wear his fashions. He told himself that he was merely caught up in the moment —the atmosphere of gaiety, excitement, and twirling color. But he suspected it was more than that.

"Too bad she's a dancer," he mused aloud. "She would look incredible in my fall line. Look at her form. Can you imagine her in that layered white silk?"

Hellyn laughed softly. "You mean too bad she's a *Gypsy* dancer. There's the rub. Many dancers would like to be models, but not Gypsy dancers. You're really dreaming tonight, York, but then that's what makes you such a splendid designer."

"What do you mean?"

17

"Gypsies don't work for *gajé* which is what all non-Gypsies are known as: outsiders. Gypsies belong to a furtive and mysterious society. That's how they've survived all these years. They even speak a secret language known as Romany to identify other Gypsies and keep *gajé* from understanding them."

"How do you know so much about them?" York asked, glancing askance at her. "Until tonight I thought they had all but vanished in the modern world."

Hellyn laughed softly. "I've always been so fascinated that I made it a point to find out what I could—precious little, I can tell you. But Gypsies are still very much alive."

York smiled. "That dancer is very much alive, no doubt about it. She's incredible."

"She's also probably married and has to answer to both a husband and a father," Hellyn told him. "They marry at a young age, usually between twelve and sixteen. Your Gypsy looks to be in her early twenties. She's probably been married for years."

"You're not serious?"

"Very," Hellyn said. "Parents still arrange marriages and pay bride prices to keep the races pure and the culture alive."

York looked back at the gorgeous dancer as she writhed and twisted sensuously. She *couldn't* be married, he told himself firmly. It would interfere with his plans. And premature though they were, he had plans.

He couldn't help but assess her possibilities as a model, and the fact that she was a Gypsy only added to her attraction. She was poised, with innate dignity

18

and carriage. And he liked her hauteur. It gave her an unapproachable look that he found challenging and appealing. She had exquisite lines and bones. She was used to performing before the public. What else could he ask for?

"I want her to model for me," he stated, as though his desire was the determining factor.

Hellyn gave him a surprised look. "Even you can't have everything you want, York. She won't do it. I told you, it's against a Gypsy's principles to work for *gajé*."

York was becoming more fascinated, and not in the least discouraged. He looked into the Gypsy dancer's dark green eyes. "She's working for *gajé* now," he observed.

Hellyn shook her head. "It isn't the same at all. She's an artist, a performer. She won't model."

"She'll model for me," York insisted. "Most women dream about modeling."

Hellyn shook her head. "Oh, York, you're so cocky. Charming, but cocky all the same. Well, don't say I didn't warn you. If you persist in such a foolish idea, she'll work for you all right. She'll take you for a ride you'll never forget."

Turning to her in amusement, York smiled. "Sounds tempting."

"You're impossible!" Hellyn exclaimed in mock agitation. "I should have known better than to invite you, but I'd heard that this woman was a dancing legend. I thought the evening might prove entertaining for you."

"Oh, it has. It has," York murmured. His gaze roved over the dancer again.

19

Shanda couldn't seem to stay away from center stage, and when she danced there, she couldn't stop looking at the *gajó*. It was an unusual predicament for her, and she was angry with both herself and him for her interest.

The mere fact that he and his companion were discussing her didn't bother her; after all, she was an entertainer, and she had learned long ago that the audience was out for an amusing time. If they were talkers by nature, they talked. As long as they weren't loud enough to disrupt her performance, she accepted that; she was used to it. Gypsies saw the dance and the music as a time for gaiety, for participation. But the man—*aye, aye, aye*—she couldn't seem to keep her mind off him!

Usually her control and concentration were total. She demanded it of herself. She had learned her lessons in life from both the Gypsy and the non-Gypsy cultures. Long ago she had determined that she would make her own laws.

The fact that she once had been *marimé*, an outcast from her own *vitsa*—her tribe—in California, remained a painful memory. She had been turned out of the society when she was seventeen for refusing to marry the boy her father preferred for her.

But she had quickly found that she was a Gypsy in her soul, and she could not abandon her heritage. She could not turn her back on her culture and people for the superficial world of the *gajé*.

She had been reinstated by her own choice, after she became famous and was able to substantially increase the leader's coffers and prestige, but the bitter

20

lesson remained, and it was understood that she would be governed by no one.

She now lived in two worlds: the Gypsy one ruled by her heart, and the *gajé* one ruled by her head. But she lived her own life, and she gave her heart to no man. There was no *rom* to rule her, to crush her heart and spirit and bind her to him as her Gypsy father had done her mother.

In the Gypsy world freedom was primarily for the man. She had learned that from her mother—her red-haired, disillusioned *gají* mother. Fleeing from her thoughts, she twisted and leapt away from the hypnotizing eyes of the stranger. She would not look at him again while she danced.

"York."

He turned back to Hellyn, hating to glance away from the dancer for even a moment. "Hmm?"

"Aren't you listening to what I'm telling you?"

He smiled. He was listening, but his heart and his eyes weren't hearing. The woman was remarkable. There was no other way to describe her.

Hellyn sighed in resignation as York looked back at the dancer without commenting. "I'm drawn to their uninhibited way of life, their songs and music and laughter," she said, glancing from York to the dark male Gypsy who played the violin. "They are very romantic, aren't they?"

She didn't expect an answer; York appeared to be mesmerized. "The trio seems an odd combination," she mused aloud. "The guitarist is probably *Gitano,* of Spanish origin, and the violinist is probably of Hungarian descent—an odd combination indeed—

21

and I don't know about the girl. She seems pure renegade."

"That sounds intriguing," York said with a grin, then watched as the lights dimmed and the dancer left the stage to resounding applause.

After taking a fifteen-minute break, the violinist returned and began a brooding melody that captured the audience with its mournful quality. Slowly, provocatively, the dancer joined the soloist. At the tips of her fingers ebony castanets quivered. She edged closer and closer to the violinist, then began to move erotically in front of him.

The lights flared suddenly and the melody became wild and joyous. Abruptly, the dancer plunged into a pagan dance that seemed especially bold after the melancholy song.

York's eyes narrowed as he saw that the woman was dressed even more provocatively now, her skirt shorter, a blouse tied seductively around her midriff, her hair long and free. Drawing in his breath, he forgot that there was anyone else in the room. As the Gypsy curved backward, her slender shoulders almost grazing the floor, he ached to reach out and stroke the dark curtain of wavy black hair which swayed with her every movement. He wanted to tangle his fingers in it and pull the woman to him so that he might taste the treasure of her red lips.

Suddenly she arched her neck until she was able to look directly into his eyes. York's heart stopped, but he felt himself responding to her with every other muscle of his body.

When the dancer slowly eased up from the floor, her movements tantalizing and sensuous, York's heart began to pound again. He could hear the pulse of his blood racing in his veins as his heart beat like a drum inside his chest.

Shanda turned to face him, wanting to stir him as he had stirred her. She began to flirt with him unabashedly, captivating him with her eyes, lowering her lashes enchantingly, luring him with her provocative movements.

Not until she saw York's eyes glaze over as though he were hypnotized did she relent. Then she turned her back to him and flirted with Vagan, the violinist, just as fervently.

"I told you she liked you," Hellyn said, breaking the spell that had bound York to the dancer.

He glanced at his friend in surprise. He had been so mesmerized by the dancer that he had forgotten where he was. In fact, he felt a tightening in his stomach that he could only describe as jealousy as he watched her work her magic on the violinist.

He laughed a little nervously. "That kind of liking could be fatal. My God, but she's intoxicating. I could feel myself respond to her with my whole body."

Hellyn laughed. "I told you she could make a fool of you with no effort. Do you get my point now?"

Again York looked at her in surprise. He *had* readily succumbed to the woman's charms, and all she had done was flirt with him. He laughed good-naturedly.

"Yes, I think I do. But I've been warned now, and I'm on guard."

"It won't do you any good. You'll have no use for armor against that one. You won't get any closer than you are now."

23

York smiled slowly. "We'll see." He wanted the Gypsy, and he wasn't one to be denied something he wanted.

He studied the whirling witch as she moved in front of him again, this time her face cold and impassive, her devotion given only to the dance. He was sure she could stir any audience; she would cause just as much of a sensation modeling as she would dancing.

As Shanda spun to a grand finale, the applause echoed in her ears. Aloud, she whispered, "Thank you, *o Del.*" She was very superstitious, and she always thanked God for a successful performance.

She bowed from the waist to the people at the left of the stage, bending down low, letting her masses of full dark hair touch the floor. Then she sauntered over and repeated the bow to the right. The applause continued unabated, and when she had gone to center stage, she met the *gajó* stranger's eyes briefly before she bowed.

When she slowly straightened, she unavoidably looked into his face once more. To her surprise he threw her a red carnation from the vase of flowers on his table. She deftly caught it, then raised it high in the air and smiled at the audience in general before she tossed her hair over one shoulder and strolled off the stage.

The musicians bowed, then followed the dancer. York watched as they all disappeared behind the black curtain. The clapping continued, but they did not return. He shifted uneasily in his chair. The woman had caught his flower. What did she mean to say by keeping it?

"Shall we go?"

He blinked his dark eyes, then looked at Hellyn. "Pardon me?"

She snapped her fingers. "The woman has you under some kind of spell," she teased. "I asked if you're ready to go."

He shook his head. "I'm going backstage. Will you go with me or wait here?"

Eyes glowing, Hellyn stood up. "I wouldn't miss this, let me assure you," she insisted. "I've never seen York Summerfield rejected. It'll be something new."

He pretended to tap her chin with his fist. "Don't gloat yet. You still haven't seen it." He leaned very near and whispered, "A thousand dollars says she'll model."

"You're on!" she cried. "Unlike you celebrities, we peons are always in need of money."

York laughed. "Peons, indeed! You own one of the best-known modeling agencies in New York, not to mention the fact that your parents left you a fortune. That's what makes you so damned independent."

She smiled at him, but she couldn't deny what he had said. "Let me see you try to charm the Gypsy, York. It'll help me sleep better to know you've been put in your place for once in your life."

Grinning, he took her arm and led her to the hall that went to the performers' dressing rooms. He had no intention of losing his wager.

CHAPTER TWO

When York knocked on the first door, the Spanish guitarist answered. "Yes?"

His hair was dark blond and his eyes were blue and smiling. He had the patrician features of an aristocrat. He looked first at York, then at Hellyn. His attention settled on the woman, and he smiled broadly.

"Can I help you?"

"I'm looking for the dancer," York said, causing the man to turn toward him.

The blond gypsy studied him swiftly, then smiled at Hellyn again. "I am Miguel," he answered smoothly, his words honeyed. "Perhaps I can help you."

"You might be able to help her," York answered impatiently, "but I'd like to know which room the dancer is in."

Slowly, audaciously, the guitarist assessed York again, letting his blue gaze rove from the expensive shoes to the dark hair. "She is not available right now."

He smiled a little tauntingly. "But she will dance again tomorrow night. Come back then." He smiled at Hellyn once more, then shut the door in their faces.

Taken aback, York stared in disbelief.

Hellyn tried to stifle her laughter. "Don't look so surprised. I did warn you. When you find the girl's room, she'll do worse."

York went to the next door and started to rap on it, but Hellyn caught his hand. "I suggest that you try the third dressing room. I suspect the two men have taken the first rooms to act as some kind of barrier for the woman."

She held his hand for a moment before she released it. "York, has it occurred to you that one of these men might be the girl's husband? May I also suggest that you proceed with a little more caution?"

Clearly it hadn't occurred to York, but he didn't want Hellyn to know that. "I'm on a business mission," he told her offhandedly.

"Business, my eye!" she exclaimed. "You've been dazzled by this woman, and your interest is purely personal."

York grinned at her. Maybe it was partly personal, but he did want the dancer to model for him. In fact, at some time in the course of her dance, he had begun to imagine his spring line. It would be pure Gypsy—all color and excitement and new life. And he wanted a real Gypsy to model it.

Taking Hellyn's advice, he went to the third door. They paused at the sound of sharp voices inside. York

27

couldn't make out the muffled words, but clearly there was an argument going on between a man and a woman. Impulsively, he rapped on the door.

The violinist answered. His dark eyes blazing, his face flushed, he glared at York for a second, then demanded, "What do you want?"

York was tempted to do the wise thing and leave, but he had never been wise in the face of danger. He looked beyond the dark Gypsy to the dancer who stood with her hands on her hips, still wearing the provocative outfit she had last danced in. Moisture glistened on her midriff and bosom, and for a moment York couldn't look away from the tantalizing woman.

She stirred something very elemental, very primitive in him, and at that moment he knew he had to have her, no matter what the cost or the circumstances. The thought disturbed him, and he glanced behind her to a dressing table where the red carnation he had given her lay.

"I'd like to speak with the lady."

"Come back tomorrow night," the violinist ordered, then he tried to slam the door.

York put his foot in the opening, effectively stopping the movement.

"Now," he said. He could feel Hellyn grow tense beside him, but he could not back down.

The musician glowered at him a moment longer, and York didn't miss the way the man's fists clenched and unclenched. York was anticipating a fight, but he hoped the man would remember that he needed his hands in good working order to earn his living.

So did he, York reminded himself, wondering if

he'd lost his mind coming here. What if this man was the dancer's husband?

The woman spoke in Romany, breaking the tension that filled the air. Then she spoke in English. "No man speaks for me, Vagan. Open the door."

Furious, the violinist flung the door wide open, then muttered in Romany to the dancer.

She responded sharply, her temper flaring, her green eyes dancing with anger.

The violinist picked up the carnation, shredded it in a dozen pieces, then shoved past York. York's gaze followed the young man until he had vanished into the next room, then he looked back at the woman.

Shanda was watching him with interest, asking herself if he were brave or foolish. Gypsies would fight at the drop of a hat, and Vagan had been pushed past that point. She was curious to see what the *gajó* would say—the *gajó* who had come to her room with his woman.

"Yes?" she said, her eyes cold and expressionless.

York tried his best to smile. "I'm York Summerfield, and this is Hellyn Anderson. I enjoyed your performance very much. I'd like to ask you to join us for a drink."

Shanda assessed him carefully. She liked his looks; he was handsome and exciting. But that was all the more reason to avoid him, as she did all outsiders.

She lifted her chin. "I'm pleased that you enjoyed the performance," she said coolly, "but I would not care to join you."

Then she picked up her purse, brushed past the startled couple, shut her dressing-room door, and sauntered down the hall.

29

The potent scent of her provocative perfume, made more powerful by her dance-heated body, sent York's senses spinning. Unthinkingly, he strode after her, grasped her arm, and whirled her around to face him.

"Why won't you have a drink with me?" he demanded. The question was neither tactful nor persuasive, and he wanted to bite his tongue for losing his cool.

Shanda jerked her arm free of his tight fingers. "You're *prikáza!*" she hissed. "Keep your hands off me." Then she spun on her heel and marched away.

Stunned, York watched as she opened the guitarist's door and slipped inside. He was still watching when the two of them came out, arm-in-arm, and knocked at the violinist's door. He joined them, and they headed down the hall. When they reached the end, Shanda glanced back briefly at York.

"Damned witch," he muttered as the threesome vanished around the corner.

Hellyn broke into laughter beside him. "I told you, York. And frankly, I'm grateful that you didn't get your head knocked off by that brooding violinist!"

For a moment York stood glowering at her, but when Hellyn stuck out her lower lip in a pouting imitation of a child who hadn't gotten what she wanted, he laughed.

"The violinist is the least of my worries. You forget that I'm a martial arts expert, my dear. I was in no danger."

Hellyn smiled knowingly. "And he probably had a knife concealed that could have put your martial arts to rest forever."

"Charming thought."

"Let's go have that drink," Hellyn urged. "I've had enough of Gypsies for the night."

"I haven't," York said. "Please have my chauffeur drive you home. I'll take a cab." Then he gave her a friendly kiss on the forehead and started running down the hall.

"York! Where are you going?" she cried, hurrying after him.

He turned back only long enough to wink at her. "Gypsy-hunting," he mouthed, and then he, too, was gone.

"Oh dear," Hellyn murmured to herself. "Oh dear, oh dear."

York dashed out onto the street just in time to see the Gypsies drive off in an old car. Boldly stepping out into the traffic, he tried to catch the next cab, but it rushed on by. He waved at the one that followed, but it was occupied.

He cursed in disappointment as he stared at the disappearing vehicle that held the Gypsies. He managed to get the next taxi, but it was too late to tail the dancer.

"Where to, buddy?" the man asked.

York struck his fist against his open palm. He had hoped to find out where she lived. "Hell," he muttered aloud.

The driver glanced back over his shoulder. "I don't go there. You got some other place in mind or not?"

York managed a brief smile, then gave the address of his plush penthouse apartment. The taxi driver pulled out into the fast-paced traffic.

The minute York stepped into his lavishly decorated living room, he poured himself a Scotch and water and tossed it down. Then he dialed a number.

"Yeah," a sleepy voice grumbled.

"Charley, York here. Listen, I want you to get me some information on a woman."

"Dammit, York, do you know what time it is?" the man on the other end of the line growled.

York looked at the gold watch on his wrist. "It's a little after midnight, but that's not why I called."

He heard a slight snicker from Charley, then a grudging, "I didn't think so. Why did you call?"

York laughed. "I told you. I want you to get some information on a woman—a Gypsy dancer who works at Sophie's Supreme Club."

There was a pause, then, "A Gypsy? Man, is this a joke? Are you high or what?"

York grinned. "Come on, Charley. This is no joke. I need that info as quickly as possible."

There was another pause. "Tonight? Are you talking about tonight?"

"Yes."

"Geez, York, you got some nerve. I run a legit business, just like you do, with real hours. Call back tomorrow."

"You run a detective agency, and I have my doubts about how legitimate it is, but that's beside the point. I want to find out everything I can about this woman. Have it for me tomorrow morning and it's worth five hundred dollars to you."

"Done."

York held the phone away from his ear and shook his head as he abruptly heard the dial tone. "Money talks. It even gets answers," he murmured, then replaced the receiver.

After pouring himself another Scotch and water, he settled into a contoured white chair and stared out at the view of Central Park. But he saw only the image of the Gypsy dancer, a whirling circle of color and enchantment, spinning around and around inside his head.

He sighed heavily. She had been damned hard on his ego, and he wasn't used to that. But it only made her all the more appealing. Hellyn had been right. He was too spoiled. Usually, women were more than willing to please him.

But the dancer had said no. She had spurned him, and he wasn't about to give up. Hellyn wasn't getting his thousand dollars. The Gypsy *was* going to model for him.

York arched his head and tossed back the last of his drink. What would it take? Like Charley, would she go for money? If he offered her enough, would she model? Oddly, the thought upset him. He didn't want to think of her being easily bought, and he realized that the challenge was part of her appeal.

Grinning slowly, he remembered how she had hissed the Romany word at him. He wondered what it meant. Suddenly he laughed aloud. Whatever it meant, he was positive it hadn't been flattering.

The phone rang right by his elbow and he picked it up. "Yes?"

He was greeted by Hellyn's cheerful laughter. "You mean no, don't you? I've been dying with curiosity, but you're home, so that means you had no success with the Gypsy."

"How can you be so sure?" York drawled. "How do you know I'm here alone?"

There was a pause on the other end of the line, then Hellyn cried, "Dammit, York! Did you get her to go home with you already?"

York grinned to himself. He wished he could tell Hellyn yes.

"No," he finally admitted.

"I knew it," she said in a smug voice.

"Just hold on," he insisted. "You haven't won the bet by a long shot. I didn't catch up with them or I probably would have the Gypsy right here with me."

"Well, keep me posted. This is one bet you've lost, friend. I'm already counting on banking that thousand."

He laughed. "Don't spend it yet. You'll need it to pay me."

Hellyn chuckled. "You are arrogant, York, but time will prove me right. Good night."

Thoughts of the Gypsy beauty still dancing in his head, York took a shower, then, naked, slid his long, lean body between the sleek coolness of navy silk sheets. And when his dreams came, the woman moved before him once more as she had on the stage.

Only this time she didn't run away when he pursued her. This time he took what he wanted, and he wanted it all.

Shanda stormed around her simply decorated apartment, spouting curses in Romany and English as Vagan stood with his arms crossed and his face full of rage.

"You're not my *rom!* Not my husband," she yelled

at him. "We're part of the Gypsy family and we're a working team, but you have no claims on me! I won't have you talking to me this way!"

Abruptly Miguel held up both hands. "Listen, I'm going. It's too hot in here for me. You two work this out for yourselves. I want no part of it."

"Miguel!" Shanda said sharply. "This affects you too. Don't run away."

He gave her a charming smile, then turned his back to her. "See that stripe? It's yellow all the way down. And I can't afford to have it damaged." He winked at her playfully. "My back, that is. Too many *gajé* women like to stroke it." He grinned at Shanda and waved. Then he was gone.

"Coward," she murmured, sighing tiredly as she watched him leave. Then she turned to Vagan in resignation.

"I'm weary of fighting with you over this, Vagan. You can't tell me what to do. I left my father's home for that reason and I will not tolerate it from you."

Suddenly Vagan's brooding dark features became vulnerable. "I love you, Shanda. You know that. Why do you treat me like you do? Why do you flirt with the *gajé*, then turn to me in the same manner?"

Shanda drew in a steadying breath and tried not to weaken under the young man's confession of love. She didn't want to hurt him, but his possessiveness was becoming oppressive. She had never encouraged him to think of her in such a way.

"Vagan, you know I don't love you. And you know that the flirting is only part of the act. I would have flirted with Miguel if he had been the one playing that song. It was in the rehearsal, remember? It moves the audience."

Unexpectedly, Vagan grasped her shoulders and pulled her nearer. "But it's not in rehearsal that you flirt with *gajó*. Why do you torment me so? Why do you cheapen yourself like that? I want you for my wife."

Shanda pulled his fingers from her shoulders and sadly shook her head. "Vagan, you must stop this. We can't keep fighting and still work together. I care for you like a brother, but I do not love you as you desire. I won't marry you—ever. You must believe me."

The urgency in her voice caused him to frown. "But there's no one else. Surely you aren't interested in a *gajó*, and I know no other Gypsy holds your heart."

Shanda closed her eyes, but when a picture of the stranger flashed across her darkened lids, she quickly opened them. "No man holds my heart, *gajó* or Gypsy."

She reached out and took Vagan's hands in hers, and when she felt them tremble, she was sorry she had touched him.

"Vagan, please find someone else. There are many Gypsy girls who would willingly give their hearts to you. Do us both a kindness and find one."

Her green eyes softened. "We can't keep on like this. Your jealousy is destroying our friendship. Please listen to me."

Suddenly Vagan grasped her long hair in his hands and pulled her forward. His dark eyes were sparking with fire as they glared into hers. Drawing her even closer, he bent his head and passionately claimed her

36

mouth. Shanda struggled free of his grasp and stepped back.

"Never," he growled. "Never. I will love you until I die." Then he spun on his heel and slammed out of her apartment.

Shanda ran her fingers through her hair, massaging her head where Vagan had pulled roughly. "Damned crazy Gypsy," she muttered unhappily. *"Dilo."*

Upset, she went to the bathroom and ran a tub of water. She added a generous dash of bubblebath, then stripped off her costume and slid in.

For a long time she lay soaking, letting her thoughts drift away from the unpleasantness with Vagan. She hated to break up the trio, but she couldn't keep working with him in the face of his possessiveness. He was inhibiting her dancing, and she could never allow that.

She closed her eyes and sighed miserably. Her life was becoming too complicated. It was time to move on. Like her Gypsy ancestors, she couldn't stand shackles. She needed to firm up her dance commitments in Los Angeles.

But the club there was expecting the three of them —the group known as Fever. She couldn't very well turn up with only Miguel.

She slipped farther down in the water, as if by doing so she could escape the memory of the angry confrontations with the musician, but his face remained in her mind, brooding and violent. Then gradually the features altered and the dark eyes danced.

"Aye, aye, aye," she muttered aloud. The *gajó*

stranger again. He was poison, just as Vagan was, and she tried desperately to shut him out of her mind. But it was like trying to tame the wanderlust in a Gypsy's soul. And that was impossible.

CHAPTER THREE

The next night when Shanda danced, she looked at the table directly in front of center stage, half expecting to see the stranger, but he wasn't there. He was on her mind as she twirled and spun, and she couldn't keep from scanning the room, looking for him. She was surprised to find that she was disappointed by his absence.

Somewhere in the back of her mind she had been sure he would show up. She could almost see his dark eyes and arrogant smile. She could still feel the hot touch of his fingers on her skin when they burned into her arm.

Turning her back to the audience, she danced with more fervor, keeping up with the wild beat, letting the music wash through her heart and soul. She could feel the tension in the audience as they responded to her volatile movements, filling the room with electricity.

When she whirled back around to end the number,

she looked into the *gajó* stranger's eyes. He had come after all! Her heart beat erratically at the sight of him as he moved closer to the stage, a huge bouquet of red roses in his hand.

He smiled at her as he held up the flowers. Shanda knew she should ignore them, but she couldn't. Her fingers touched York's as she leaned down and looked into his dancing eyes, and the spark of fire that flared between them was stronger than any electricity she had created with her dance.

She took the flowers, stood up, and acknowledged the applause of the audience, but she could not keep her eyes off the man in front of her. Vagan and Miguel joined her in a bow, and she could feel Vagan's hostility when he took her hand, but she ignored it. She was foolishly giddy at the sight of the stranger. She had been afraid she would never see him again.

As the three performers ran off the stage, the accolades of the audience echoed in their ears. By the time Shanda reached her dressing room, York was there, leaning carelessly against the door.

Shanda's gaze ran quickly over him, and she couldn't help but notice how appealing he was in gray slacks and a silver shirt which had an open neck revealing curling dark hair. He had magnetism and confidence that drew her to him, in spite of the danger she sensed in the attraction.

"Good evening," he said warmly. "York Summerfield, remember? I hope you like the flowers."

Shanda lowered her dark lashes to look at the deep red roses. "They're beautiful. Thank you."

Her heart was pounding. It had been one thing to think she wouldn't see him again, and quite another to have him here, standing so near, smiling so seductively.

"Will you have that drink with me tonight?"

Drawn by the desire to spend time with him, yet aware of the foolishness of such a desire, Shanda battled with herself as she slowly raised her lashes. Before she could refuse, Vagan stepped between her and the handsome man.

"Go away!" he ordered bitingly. "No decent Gypsy woman would be seen with a *gajó* man!"

Shanda sucked in her breath sharply. What Vagan had said was all too true, but she would not let him speak for her. She had to make him understand that he had no right to be so possessive.

"It's all right, Vagan," she said in English. "York and I have a date."

Vagan's face was distorted with anger as he turned to look at her, but Shanda brushed past him and entered her dressing room. She glanced back at York and motioned for him to follow.

He stepped inside and closed the door behind him. "I was afraid there was going to be trouble from your boyfriend," he said, "but I'm pleased you're going out with me."

To his surprise Shanda lay the roses on her dressing table then whirled around to face him, her hands on her hips, her bosom heaving. She had been raised to respect Gypsy men, to obey them, and the lessons still lingered in her mind, despite the fact that she didn't always agree with them.

"There will be no trouble," she declared. "Vagan was right. No decent Gypsy woman would be seen with a *gajó* man, and I will not go out with you. I'm

41

flattered by your interest and I appreciate the flowers, but there will be no more to it than that. I told Vagan I had a date with you only to put him in his place."

Stunned, York moved closer.

"Won't you reconsider?" he murmured. "I'd like very much for you to go out with me."

"No," she said firmly.

"Why?" York asked, his dark eyes roving over her beautiful face.

Unwilling and unable to explain the complexities of her life, Shanda shook her head and glanced away.

"Only one drink," York coaxed smoothly, but he was feeling an unusual sense of desperation. He didn't like being rebuffed, and he really did want to get to know this woman. She was rare and appealing —all emotion, feeling, and spirit, with a fierce pride she hid behind like a mask. She would bring a freshness, an unexplored quality to his world.

Charley had investigated quickly and thoroughly. With a paid informant, he had been sure he had gathered accurate information.

York had been told that Shanda Nicholas wasn't married, that she did, in fact, seem to be a Gypsy renegade, as Hellyn had so aptly described her. She had a Gypsy father and a *gaji* mother. Her mother had been turned out of the Gypsy tribe when her daughter was fourteen. Shanda had left on her own three years later and made a life for herself.

She had often been seen in the company of men, primarily the two Gypsies, but she seemed to be involved with no single man. The possibility existed that she had married in a Gypsy ceremony which was never recorded with state officials, but the chance seemed slim in her case. Apparently she had run away rather than marry the boy chosen for her.

Shanda shook her head, causing the long, luxurious hair to shimmer in the lamplight. "No, thank you. Not even one drink."

Smarting from her rejection, York reached out and captured her face in his hands so that she was forced to look up at him.

"Why?" he challenged softly, his gaze holding hers. "Are you afraid of me—or is it the musician?"

Shanda laced her fingers in his and pulled them from her face. Then she straightened to her full five feet nine inches.

"I'm afraid of no one! Especially no pretty *gajó* man who comes to my room one night with a woman and the next night with flowers," she said disdainfully, her dark green eyes glittering.

York was amused, rather than affronted. "Oh, is that so? And do you really think I'm pretty?" He grinned slowly.

Shanda glanced at him suspiciously, her jade eyes questioning from beneath dark lashes. She had used the term pretty as a mockery, but now she was becoming wary of this man. He was handsome, he was charming, and he was probably wealthy too. But a man too interested in his own looks . . .

York laughed deeply, then drew the surprised dancer tightly against him. "Don't worry, Gypsy lady, I'm not in love with myself. I'm much more interested in exciting women."

Before she could gather her wits about her, he lowered his head and captured her mouth with his.

43

Shanda sought to free herself from his embrace, but it was already too late. His lips burned against hers with a fire she had found in no other man.

He was skilled in the ways of love; the pleasure she found in his kiss and the hard pressure of his body against hers were simply too thrilling to ignore. He ignited the fire in her, the fire ever smoldering just beneath the surface.

York was the one to end the kiss and gaze down into her eyes, though he still held her in his arms. "I knew you would be like this, all heat and flame. I told Hellyn the first time I saw you that a man could get burned by your fire."

Abruptly Shanda jerked free of his arms and slapped his face. She had not forgotten how the *gajó* and the blond woman had laughed when she danced last night. She was no joke, no piece of conversation to amuse him and his friends.

"Now go back and tell your woman how the fire in my hand feels," she ordered, tossing her hair over her shoulder with a careless movement. "Get out of my room before I call Vagan and have him throw you out."

Baffled, York stroked his face as he stared at her. "What kind of game are you playing?" he demanded.

Green sparks flared in her eyes. "The same kind you are. Now we've both had our fun. Get out!"

Her hand was trembling when she pointed to the door. She should have known better than to let this man into her room, no matter what excuse she gave herself. He saw her like all outsiders did—a vagrant Gypsy woman who would be exciting to bed once or twice just to see if the myths about her restless, hot blood were valid.

Well, what did *gajé* know? They were too foolish and naive to realize that Gypsies were Rom, the real people. It was the Rom who knew how to live and enjoy life, not the *gajé* who spent their lives worrying about how to keep their possessions safely locked inside their houses.

York tried his best to remain calm, but his temper was rising as fast as hers. "Do you belong to Vagan or not? Why did you let me come in here? Why did you let me kiss you?"

"I told you I let you come in because I wanted to make a point to Vagan," she told him flatly. "He thinks he owns me, but no man does—or will. And I let you kiss me because I felt like it."

York's dark eyes glowed. "So, you used me to make your boyfriend jealous?"

"I would not do that. He's not my boyfriend."

York slowly smiled. "Then what's the problem? Was the kiss so bad that you had to slap me?"

"Don't laugh at me," Shanda demanded with a haughty lift of her chin. "I let no man laugh at me."

"I'm sure you don't," York murmured. "And I'm not laughing at you. I'm laughing at myself. Let your guard down a little. Come with me for a drink—for dinner, for whatever. I want to get to know you. I find you fascinating. I want to talk to you."

Shanda considered herself an expert at reading people. She had been taught the art from childhood. Most of the females in the Gypsy tribes earned the family money *dukkering*—telling fortunes—and she had been expected to do the same.

45

A good reading came from reading the person as much as the cards. But she couldn't seem to read this man. What was his motive? Oh, she knew that she was attractive, and she knew that men found her very sexy when she danced. But what did this man want from her? To talk, he had said. But he had already kissed her. When the kisses came, talk was usually the last thing on a man's mind.

"What about your blond woman?"

"She's only a friend."

Shanda looked into his face. She knew she should refuse his request and never see him again. He had a magnetism that drew her fast and hard, and she knew desire could be dangerous.

But she had faced danger before, and she was not afraid. Long ago she had taken charge of her own life, and she knew how to fend for herself. Her personality, like her background, was based on two cultures. From her mother she had learned to be cautious to survive; but that side of her nature was offset by her zest for life, her thrill for adventure, which she had inherited from her Gypsy father.

Besides, she would dance here for only one more week, and then she would go to California. And this York Summerfield interested her. She would take what pleasure she chose from him, then leave him behind her as a memory. It was the Gypsy way. Ever seeking the next sunrise, ever taking the beauty that was to be had today, and ever remembering the sweet flaming sunsets of yesterday. York would be a potent sunset to remember long after she had gone.

"Just one drink," he repeated. "I've heard about your exclusive society, but I only want a few minutes of your time. In fact, I have a business proposition for you."

He saw the suspicious look in her eyes. "Who are you?" she demanded. "Are you one of those opportunistic New York agents who hopes to make money off me? And do you think you can convince me to be your fool with kisses and flowers?"

York shook his head. He had resorted to trying to charm her. But he had wanted to kiss those full lips very badly, and he had acted without conscious thought.

"It's nothing like that. Come and listen. That won't hurt you, will it?"

Shanda scrutinized him boldly. No, it wouldn't hurt her. She would never let him hurt her.

"All right," she agreed. "One drink."

York's face lit up. "Good. You've made me one happy man tonight."

She shrugged her shoulders and thought to herself that it obviously took very little to make him happy.

"Give me a few minutes to change," she said. She gestured to the chair at her vanity table. "Sit down. I'll only be a moment."

"Fine."

York studied his surroundings while Shanda slipped a robe and outfit off a hanger and entered a bathroom off to one side of the room. The quarters were tastefully done, but better designed for a man.

Again York thought of Hellyn saying that the two Gypsy musicians probably acted as a barrier for the woman. He frowned. Getting her to model was going to be more complex than he had suspected.

His frown deepened. For several minutes he was

lost in his thoughts. He glanced up when Shanda stepped from the bathroom.

"It's steamy in there," she said by way of explanation. "I'll have to begin dressing here, or the shower will have done no good."

"Don't mind me," York said, fully enjoying the view.

Shanda had donned the thin robe that clung tightly to her damp skin. She took the pins from her hair and shook it out, letting the wavy black masses spill around her face and down her shoulders.

As she reached for her hairbrush, she thought of all the restrictions she had been reared with. In the Gypsy world the sexes were kept separated until marriage; a woman wasn't even supposed to brush her hair in front of a man.

She shook her head and smiled at how far she had strayed from her childhood teachings, and yet she knew they lingered in her mind. Almost in defiance of all that she had left behind, she picked up the brush and began to stroke her hair, knowing that York would watch her.

She was right, of course. He couldn't stop staring. There was only a single light on the dressing table. It silhouetted the dark beauty, giving her ethereal qualities, and York drew in his breath, wondering if she had any idea how she affected him.

Her slender hand moved the brush through the masses of shimmering hair, and York watched as the waves fell back into place like black satin. The sight of her was so erotic that he couldn't look away.

"You're very beautiful," he murmured involuntarily.

Shanda paused in front of the mirror and met his eyes reflected there. For no reason she could fathom, her heart began to beat wildly. Her lips parted, ready to toss off a casual "thank you" for the compliment she had often heard, but she seemed hypnotized by the dark stranger in her mirror.

She swallowed and looked away. "I think the steam is gone. I can dress now. Excuse me."

For the first time in her life she was self-conscious as she returned to the bathroom. She had wanted to provoke York, but in doing so, she had somehow disturbed herself. She dressed quickly, eager to leave the upsetting sensations behind her, but she soon saw that it wouldn't be possible.

When she entered the room, clothed in a simple peasant blouse cut low and tied at her waist, a full skirt with large pockets, and ballet shoes laced at the ankles, York's eyes glowed with a strange fire.

"I'm ready."

York nodded. "You are indeed." He had an urge to cross the room, pull her into his arms, and lose himself in her beauty, but he restrained himself.

"I know a secluded place with music, good food and drinks. Will that be all right?"

Shanda nodded. "I'm sure it will."

She shouldn't have been surprised when York took her hand and led her out to a chauffeured car. But she was both surprised and disappointed. His different dress and careless manner had led her to believe that he was the exception to the rich playboys she studied from her vantage point on the club stage. She had always avoided them. She really knew nothing

49

about this man, and instinct told her to proceed with care.

"A nice car," she commented lightly when the chauffeur had assisted her into the backseat and York had joined her. "What do you do for a living? Rob banks?"

York laughed. "Nothing so dangerous. I'm afraid I spend my time designing clothes."

"Designing clothes?" Shanda was taken aback. "You mean you sew?" She made her own clothes and her costumes for dancing, but she couldn't imagine a man doing that.

York's deep laughter filled the car. "I have in my day, to learn the business from the bottom up, but that's not what I do now. I come up with ideas for clothes which someone else sews."

"You're a fashion designer—like Calvin Klein or Ralph Lauren?" she asked, dismayed. It had never occurred to her.

Smiling, York said, "Yes, we're all fashion designers, but I have very different ideas and clothing. All my life I've admired beautiful women and wanted to dress them as appealingly as possible." He smiled seductively. "I still love doing that, but I love undressing them even more."

Shanda glanced at him out of the corner of her eye. She was sure he had undressed plenty of women in his time.

York sobered when she didn't laugh at his little joke. "Seriously, I love my work, and I've gained some respect in the business. In fact, I've won the Coty Award twice."

"The Coty Award?"

York groaned and shook his head. This woman was going to be very hard on his ego, very hard indeed. Clearly his fashion credentials weren't going to help.

"It's the fashion world's equivalent of the Oscar," he explained.

"I see," she said.

But it was all too plain that she neither saw nor cared. York grinned to himself. How refreshing she was. How beautiful. And how challenging. He was sure she would set the fashion world on its ear.

CHAPTER FOUR

Shanda had expected York to take her to some elite restaurant in the swanky part of the city, and she was delighted when he led her into a cavernous old building on a back street filled with noise and laughter.

When they entered the dark interior, a waiter dressed in a Cossack uniform motioned for them to follow him to a rough-hewn table at the back of the room.

There were few diners at this late hour, but Shanda could hear boisterous shouts and echoes of music coming from down the hall. The walls vibrated with the effects of unrestrained revelry and rough voices speaking in an oddly familiar, yet foreign language.

This was the last place she had expected York to frequent, and she waited in amused anticipation to see what he would do and say next.

"Vodka?" he asked, as if it were the most natural thing in the world.

A small smile played at the corners of Shanda's full

lips. She was a little doubtful about drinking strong liquor with this man. She was sure to lose her inhibitions and that could be risky, but she was betting that she could drink the fiery Russian brew as well as this *gajó* aristocrat.

"Wonderful," she said. "I like vodka."

The arching of York's brow was almost imperceptible. He was hoping that he could break down some of the Gypsy's walls here in this very basic, unique atmosphere. Yet he wasn't sure.

He suspected it would be difficult for either of them to keep up pretenses here. Between the vodka and the people, barriers were quickly broken. He had discovered that the first time he stumbled upon the place on a night when he desperately needed a distraction.

York motioned to the waiter, and he reappeared at once with thick, short glasses full of the potent brew. When they had been served, and the bottle left on the table, York held up his glass to Shanda.

"To us. May this be only the first of many such nights."

His dark eyes were glittering, luring Shanda nearer and nearer. She touched glasses with him and smiled, but she did not comment on the toast.

The vodka burned all the way down her throat, and she sipped delicately while York smiled at her in the flickering lamplight. Already she could feel herself warming to him, even as the vodka warmed her throat.

"Shall I order dinner for us both, or do you insist on doing that yourself?" he asked, his voice teasing.

Shanda shrugged. "That depends on what you suggest. Perhaps I might not like it."

York laughed at her blunt response. *"Pirojok."*

Shanda took another sip of her vodka and pretended to consider, then consented. She suspected that York thought she didn't know what the dish was, but she knew it well. She'd had the meat-filled pastry served with soup occasionally when she dined with Russian Gypsies.

The waiter reappeared and York ordered their meal. Shanda leaned back against the well-worn cushions of her chair and smiled secretly to herself. She had expected this man to try to impress her, but now she didn't know what to think.

Did he know that she had no interest in material things—in power and money and all the trappings the *gajé* equated with success? Was that why he had brought her here to this place that was surely alien to him?

She smiled again. "You would make a good Gypsy *rom baró,* a group leader." A *rom baró* was wise enough to control men with his words, and women would obey him for only a smile.

Abruptly she straightened in her chair. Such foolish thoughts were dangerous to express. She wanted to give him no sense of power.

"Do you really think so?" York murmured.

Shanda shrugged casually. She had already said too much, and she refused to endanger herself further just to build up his ego.

Across the table, York stared at her intently. "What are you thinking?"

She shook her head, and the masses of dark hair

swayed around her heart-shaped face. "Nothing, really." She looked down at her glass and toyed with the thick base.

Unexpectedly York reached across the table and took her hands in his. "Open up to me, sweet Shanda. Talk to me. Tell me about your mysterious life and secret smiles. I want to know all about you."

She blinked wide eyes as she met his penetrating gaze. "How do you know my name?"

York could feel the collar of his shirt tightening. Charley had told him, of course.

He shrugged. "Didn't you tell me?"

Shanda didn't recall doing so, but then she had behaved unwisely with this man from the first moment she met him. "I don't believe I did."

York laughed lightly. "A name isn't so much to know. I want to hear more."

Shanda looked at the pools of shadowy light made by the flickering flame of the lamp. She was reminded of long ago nights when her *kumpania* had met on riverbanks in northern California and staged dances and feasts around blazing campfires.

She pushed at the memory. It all seemed so distant now. "There's nothing that would interest you," she said.

He squeezed her long fingers, and Shanda felt a rush of fire that seemed to burn right to her heart. "Tell me what goes on inside that pretty head of yours."

He wasn't trying to deceive her. He wanted her to model, it was true, but when he looked into those green eyes, he wanted more than anything to make some kind of intimate contact with this woman. He began to stroke the sensitive skin of her hands with his thumbs, and Shanda drew away.

"I'm a Gypsy dancer. What you see is what I am."

"I like what I see," he murmured in a husky voice. "But I know there's more here than the lovely, talented dancer."

Shanda took another drink of the vodka, then laughed aloud, the sound rich and shimmering. "You have the sugary tongue of a Gypsy, York Summerfield. Is that how you got so far in dress designing—romancing the ladies?"

It was the first time York had heard her laugh, and her laughter warmed him as no brilliant flash of sunshine ever had. He thought she was beginning to feel comfortable with him at last, and he didn't realize until he leaned back against his chair how tense he had been.

He grinned at her. "I love the ladies, all right, but my success is my own. It took years of study at the Fashion Institute of Technology, an enormous amount of initiative and originality on my part."

He gazed steadily at her despite the reflections of the lamplight that caused her green eyes to shimmer. "And what about you? Where did you learn to dance so fantastically?"

She took another sip of biting vodka. "All Gypsies are born to dance. We learn at our mothers' knees."

York studied her speculatively for a moment. "That might be, but all Gypsies don't end up dancing in a chic place like Sophie's Supreme Club. How did that happen?"

She looked away from him, unwilling to share her

past with a stranger. "Destiny, I suppose. Our fates are predetermined, are they not?"

He grinned. "Are they? Is that what you believe?"

She lowered her head, wondering if he was laughing at her.

As though he sensed her further withdrawal, York coaxed, "Tell me what you do with your days. Tell me about the nights that you don't dance. What are your goals, your ambitions, your dreams?"

"Tell me about yours," she said, meeting his interested gaze.

"I want to keep designing clothes as long as I can see, think, and draw. It's been my desire since I was a teenager, and I can't imagine not doing it. Success has only made me more ambitious. I keep trying to better myself, to top my last achievement."

"Why? Because of the money?"

"That's part of it," he admitted. "But the personal satisfaction is a bigger part."

He laughed a little uneasily when he realized that he was talking about himself, but she had avoided telling him anything.

"Have you ever been married?" he asked, knowing the question was prompted by his knowledge that she had refused to marry the boy her father had chosen. He thought it might encourage her to open up to him.

She averted her gaze to trace the tines of her fork. "No, have you?"

He smiled. "Oh, I've considered it a couple of times, but I haven't found the right woman."

"And what's right?" she asked, her eyes penetrating as they met his.

He was pensive for a moment. "I guess I'd have to say that I want a woman who will support me in whatever I do. A helpmate, to use an archaic expression. I also want a woman who wants children. That's very important to me, and no longer guaranteed in this day and age."

Shanda nodded. So he *would* make a good Gypsy. He wanted a woman in chains while he remained free.

"Do you want children?" he asked, breaking into her thoughts.

"Yes." She didn't add that she didn't believe marriage was a prerequisite for having them. But she did believe love was, and she was well aware that York hadn't mentioned love.

"Have you heard of love?" she couldn't resist asking, but her voice was full of deceptive lightness and her smile was teasing.

"Yes, of course. I can't imagine a world without it. Can you?"

"No."

York nodded slowly. He realized that the conversation had ended—what little conversation there had been. He had been too optimistic. She wasn't going to open up to him yet. He still knew little about her.

"Where did you get those incredible green eyes?" he asked, changing the subject. "I was under the impression that Gypsies were dark-eyed and dark-skinned."

Shanda leaned forward, resting her elbows on the table, unaware that the pose exposed the curve of her breasts in the low-cut blouse.

York tried his best to keep his gaze on her face as she talked, but he found her achingly tempting.

"Gypsies are of all colors and textures. We might have come from India originally, but Gypsies who arrived here after the Second World War came from all over Europe."

York was entranced by her uniqueness, her pride, her beauty. "How extraordinary you are, Shanda. You enchant me."

She took another sip of vodka, gazing at him over the rim of the glass. He enchanted her, too, and therein lay the danger.

"Your tongue is very sweet," she said when she had set her glass down. "You've made it an art to seduce women, have you not?"

Taken aback, York took a long drink of his vodka, then refilled his glass. His laughter was low and brief. "My God, I hope not. Do I seem that transparent to you?"

Shanda looked straight into his eyes. "Yes."

For a moment York simply stared at her. Then he smiled. "Do you tell fortunes, too, Gypsy woman? Can you look into my future and see that I'm a cad who means you nothing but harm?"

Shanda never looked into the future, hers or anyone else's. She wanted to savor each day, to make the most of each experience, to live every moment. And most of all she wanted to stay free and dance.

She smiled. "I can see that you and I have no future at all," she said simply. She could say it in all honesty, because she would never allow it, no matter how much he appealed to her.

Now it was York's turn to lean forward and stare at

his drink. He fervently hoped that she had no real power to see the future, for he meant for her to play a prominent part in his.

"I see," he said at last, and he was grateful when their meal was served. He was suddenly very reluctant to ask her to model for him, afraid that she would refuse.

There was silence for a few moments while they ate. "Tell me about the two musicians who play for you," he said finally. "The violinist is surely in love with you." A teasing look came into his eyes. "Or is that merely the way all men respond to you?"

Shanda's full lips parted in a slow, challenging smile, and her eyes immobilized him so that he couldn't look away even if he had wanted to. "Is that how you respond to me?"

Of course he wasn't in love with her, but he seemed almost fatally fascinated. Somewhere inside him, he felt that he absolutely had to have her—if only for a brief time.

He laughed a little nervously. "I confess that you have me under your spell. I don't quite know what to think of you, and you aren't making it any easier."

Shanda stroked her glass in a seductive gesture. "Isn't that the best way? Keep a man guessing? Keep the mystery and the allure in the relationship?"

York thought the woman might drive him mad. He reached across the table and stilled her fingers with his. "Are we going to have a relationship, Shanda?"

"No," she said, and York was immediately sorry he had asked. She sounded so definite. Her eyes were solemn. "You asked me to come here to talk about a business proposition. What is it?"

York weighed his chances of convincing her to model, and decided the scale definitely wasn't balanced in his favor. In fact, he might ruin any chance he had to see her again if he asked.

"That can wait until another time. There's dancing here in the back room. I think we should go and watch. I believe you'll like it."

Shanda was curious about his business proposition, but she would not ask again. Maybe he had changed his mind. Perhaps he had realized that what he had intended would insult her. If so, she didn't want to know about it.

She could hear the fast-paced, exotic melody from the back room, and it lured her with its teasing call. Music was much better than business any day.

She rose and let York take her hand to guide her into a big, bare room reserved for dancing and drinking. Two Cossack costumed men strolled around the floor playing for men who danced madly, laughing and near-drunk as they kicked and moved with amazing dexterity and balance. Many people thronged around the lively dancers, clapping and offering encouragement.

The atmosphere was wildly infectious, and York saw Shanda's green eyes glow. He had suspected she would come to life here among these people and the music. They were Russian immigrants, basic and earthy. Many of the women dressed in a similar fashion to Shanda, though others were dressed more elaborately.

York smiled to himself. No one here knew or cared who he was or what money he made. He was nothing to them. They wanted only to drink and dance and live life. He envied them in a way, for he was trapped by his own ambitions. Making his mark had been important; staying at the top counted. And Shanda could help keep him there.

He was amazed to hear her suddenly call out something in Romany. The music stopped and everyone in the room turned to look at her.

She spoke again, and one of the musicians rushed over to embrace her. There were shouts and cries of recognition, and much hand-clasping and boisterous laughter.

"Shanda, the legendary Gypsy dancer," one of the dark, bearded men said loudly in English to anyone who might not have known. "Shanda, the Gypsy renegade who knows all Gypsy people as her own, regardless of race."

Then he whispered something to her and she was quickly ushered out onto the floor with the men. She glanced at York only once as he stood on the sidelines, bewildered.

Shanda smiled to herself. These were Russian Gypsies and York hadn't even known it. She experienced a sudden rush of empathy for him. He was in a foreign world, and she knew how that could be. She lived in cross-cultures, totally belonging in neither, making her own way.

The music began again, and she didn't want the *gajó* stranger to dominate her heart and thoughts. She was weary of wondering about him. She wanted only to respond to the beat in her blood, the throbbing in her veins, the stimulating lure of the balalaika.

Impulsively she cried out in joy and lifted her skirts

high to move to the exhilarating notes. The others gathered around her and clapped and called out encouragement in Romany, and Shanda was transformed as she spun before the crowd.

She loved to dance, and she loved an audience. Tonight she especially wanted York to see the dance as it should be, among the people who understood *duende:* feeling, emotion—the real life of movement —as no other people on earth.

Lost to the rhythms inside her, she leapt and whirled, her mouth open in laughter, her hair damp and flying, the blood pounding at her temples. The vodka had gone to her head, and she danced with an abandon, a wildness, a recklessness that spoke of unbridled passion, of untamed desire.

York, his heart hammering, stood by, hypnotized by the spinning Gypsy. She was splendid. She was like a mythical creature making magic with her body and her laughter, causing the crowd to cheer her on.

Suddenly the music changed, and other people joined the laughing Shanda on the floor. As though obsessed, York followed them. Uncaring of the tempo or the foreign steps, he pulled her into his arms.

She continued to move enticingly to the music, her hands lifting up the masses of her hair. But she was aware of York's powerful presence. In fact, the heady sensation of being in his arms was so potent that for a moment she thought she might be engulfed by it.

Leaning into him in a way that let her feel every hard muscle, she wrapped her arms around his neck and gazed up into his eyes as the sad-sweet melody surrounded them.

York moved closer, his breath warm on her cheek

as he whispered, "You do something crazy to me, Shanda. I don't even know you, but I can't get you out of my head."

Tinkling laughter spilled from her lips at the idea of him echoing her own thoughts. York caught the laughter with his lips and kissed it from her mouth.

"Don't laugh at me, Gypsy. I'm serious."

Shanda felt that she shared some strange kinship with this man who had unknowingly taken her among her own kind, and she laughed again.

"I can't help it. I've thought the same thoughts you have. I think we're both *dilo*—crazy. We've known each other two days. We're from different cultures with different values. We *are* mad to be here at all."

York smiled at her. "You've cast a spell on me, and when you've finished with me, I'm afraid you'll vanish into the sunset in a Gypsy caravan."

Shanda sobered. She *would* vanish; she would go away next week just as surely as the sun rose and the sun set. She felt strangely unhappy at the thought. But they had the moment, and that was all anyone could ask for.

"You speak like the *gajó* charmer you are," she said gently. "What are you promising me after tonight?"

York looked startled. He didn't know. "What can I promise that would please you?" he asked with a lightness he was far from feeling. "Fame? Success? More money than you've ever imagined?"

Shanda shook her head. "All fleeting," she admonished with a husky laugh. "The spirit and the heart are what count. And you aren't offering me either, are you?"

York was thoroughly confounded by her question as he looked into her lovely face.

Shanda smiled knowingly. "Don't look so distressed, York. I don't want your promises. I'm a Gypsy, remember? I know the empty value of pretty words."

Fortunately the music ended, and with it, the strange spell that had been woven around him. "Let's have another drink," he said.

"Fine."

As they walked back to the other room, she said, "You didn't know that the musicians were Gypsies, did you?"

York shook his head and grinned. "No wonder I thought you'd like it here."

She gazed into his eyes. "Yes, it was a good choice. I've had a wonderful time."

When they returned to the table, York ordered *kissel*, puree of cranberries served with cream, and *café russe*, coffee with Russian vodka.

As the night wore on, they laughed and talked, but they did not dance again, nor did they discuss anything of significance. York hoped that another night, another time they might.

He had seen the passionate woman beneath the shield, and he liked what he saw. He would wait and see what developed. It was a difficult task for a man used to having what he wanted.

Finally a waiter came to tell them the restaurant was closing. York looked at Shanda in surprise.

"I didn't realize it was so late," he said, glancing at his watch.

So, the night was coming to an end. She wondered

what would happen now. Would he try to kiss her, to go home with her, to see her again? She pushed the thoughts to the back of her mind. The real question was what would *she* do?

CHAPTER FIVE

When the chauffeured car had delivered them to her address, Shanda didn't have time to ponder her alternatives. York helped her out of the car and told the driver, "Pick me up in half an hour."

She watched as the car drove off, then faced York with a faint smile. "And what if I don't let you in?"

He laughed softly as he took her arm and led her up the steps to the door of the brownstone. "Then I'll stand out under the stars and seduce you for all the neighbors to see."

"Perhaps I won't allow even a kiss," she insisted, thinking him terribly sure of himself.

Before she could speak again, York drew her into his arms. "I think you will."

His mouth claimed hers in a hungry, possessive kiss, and Shanda knew in that moment that she had wanted this all evening. His lips moved against hers, teasing and coaxing, burning and stirring the hot coals that had simmered inside her since he had first touched her. She felt breathless.

She wanted to forget all the things she had feared about being in a man's arms—the danger, the doubt, the heartache—but most of all, the fear of being bound by her own desire. And it was all too easy to forget in York's arms. It was with great restraint that she turned away from his tantalizing lips.

When she glanced at the next apartment, she saw a movement behind the curtained window. Vagan and Miguel lived there with friends, which was a common Gypsy practice. They hadn't wanted to rent a place for themselves because they knew the New York tour would last less than three months.

Her eyes met Vagan's and she quickly looked away. He was volatile and hot tempered, and she didn't want him to spoil this night.

"I think I should invite you in," she murmured in a husky voice. Even as she said it, she knew she shouldn't. She really hadn't meant to let him any further into her world.

With trembling fingers she unlocked the door and led the way in. When she had turned on a light, she looked back to catch the expression on York's face when he saw the room.

"What happened here?" he asked, looking at the open single room. From the outside appearance of the house, he had expected at least two bedrooms. Now only the bathroom was intact.

Shanda laughed at the typical *gajé* reaction.

"It's the Gypsy way to tear down as many inside walls as possible and to remove all the doors."

"Why?" he asked, frowning.

"It's tradition," she said. "Perhaps it originates from the days of the tent and wagon, and most of all, the Gypsy desire not to be hemmed in."

"Did you do this?"

Shanda smiled and shook her head. "Some long ago Gypsy tenant did it. Once it happens, a house more or less becomes Gypsy grounds, for word is passed among the Rom that a particular area is now habitable."

Shanda watched the surprise move over York's face. She wished she could read his mind as he glanced around the enormous room, noting the tapestry-covered walls, the bright-colored furniture, and the thick Persian rug. The kitchen was separated by a wrought-iron divider, but the canopied bed and living room looked like one big sitting room. Although immaculate, the living quarters were far from luxurious.

He walked over to a busy tapestry that portrayed the bright color and movement of a Gypsy wedding feast. "This is beautiful," he said, running his hands over the material.

Because he worked with fabric, he appreciated the fine texture, and he couldn't resist touching it. But more than that, he stood before the colorful confusion of silk and wool seeking some clue to Shanda's emotions.

"I rented this furnished," Shanda said, breaking into his thoughts, "but the tapestries are mine. I take them everywhere with me."

York glanced at the bright furniture and the Persian rug, then his eyes strayed to the wrought-iron divider that separated the kitchen from the bedroom.

"I've never seen anything quite like it," he said.

"The place suits my needs," she commented, and she wondered what it took to suit his. She imagined that he lived in a plush home with all the trappings and burdens of his wealth.

"Do you want a cup of coffee?" she asked.

York's attention focused on her once again; she fit so beautifully into her surroundings. With her shining black hair, bright jade eyes, honey-gold skin, and ruby lips, she seemed to reflect the many colors in the room. Dressed in clothes that echoed those worn by the Gypsies in the tapestry, she could have stepped right out of its brightly colored background.

He shook his head. "What I really want is you," he whispered, drawing her back into his arms. He was eager to know the heat of her body and the beating of her heart against his again.

Shanda trembled as her hips molded tightly to his and her breasts throbbed where they made contact with his solid chest. She felt as if she were drowning inside, and she could find no safe harbor to cling to as his mouth closed down on hers passionately.

York groaned as his hands traced the tantalizing curves of the woman in his arms. Her body was superb, and he couldn't seem to get enough of the feel of her beneath his mouth and fingertips. His lips left hers to scatter hot kisses along the length of her slender neck, and when she arched her head, he trailed his moist tongue down to the pulsing spot at the base of her throat.

Shanda moaned, thinking she should stop this madness while there was still time, but she couldn't make herself draw away. York's mouth was hot and searching on her sensitive skin, and when he teasingly traced the exposed curve of her bosom, she shivered. With skilled fingers he untied the knot of her blouse and slipped his hands under the loose material to caress the curve of her breasts.

"Don't," she whispered in a voice that was almost pleading.

York raised his head, and when he saw the look in her eyes, he straightened. The last thing he wanted to do was draw away, but he couldn't continue in the face of her genuine plea. He exhaled heavily and ran shaking hands through his straight black hair as she retied her blouse, her eyes lowered, her long lashes shadowy against her dusky skin.

He drew in a deep breath. "May I see you tomorrow night?"

Shanda didn't look up; she seemed engrossed in the ties of her blouse, and didn't reply at once. She wanted to refuse, but couldn't seem to find the words.

York's nerves were on edge; his body was burning; he wanted her.

"I want to call you."

She shook her head.

Involuntarily, York reached out and touched her chin with a single finger. "Why not?" he murmured.

"I don't have a phone," she answered.

The simple and unexpected explanation caused him to laugh in relief. "Then just tell me I can come for you tomorrow night at seven," he said. When Shanda hesitated, he added, "Please."

71

She searched his eyes, lured by the plea in his husky voice.

"Come backstage after the performance next Saturday night," she said at last, knowing that she was a fool.

Something would not let her send him away forever. She would have an entire week to marshal her defenses, she thought, and would be able to see him once more without giving too much of herself.

York didn't want to wait a week, but he sensed the danger in pressing this elusive woman. Perhaps he could use the time to find a way to reach her.

"All right," he agreed. Then he tangled his fingers in her long hair and pulled her to him for a final kiss.

"Good night, Shanda. Sleep well." Then without another word, he turned and left her.

Shanda stared after him for a long time. His touch had left her aching and unfulfilled, but he was *prikáza*—bad luck; she was sure of it. And *gajé* bad luck at that! She knew she wouldn't sleep well, not with York's face always before her, heating her blood with the memory of his searing kiss.

Sitting in the posh studio in his apartment, York sipped brandy as he thought of Shanda. Like the rich, fiery liquor in his glass, the Gypsy dancer spun around and around in his head.

The phone rang, startling him from his thoughts, and he answered with a brusque "Hello."

"Oh, dear," Hellyn teased on the other end of the line. "Things must not be going well for you to speak so gruffly."

York snapped, "Hellyn, it's the middle of the night. What do you want?"

"How about my thousand dollars?" she teased. "Or have you wrought some miracle?"

He was worried that it would take a miracle to ever get Shanda out of his mind. "No, I haven't, but I'm working on it."

"Poor York," Hellyn sympathized. "I told you that Gypsy would take you for a merry ride. You'd better direct your energy to your spring line instead. Let her dance right on out of your life and stick with conventional models before she tramples your creative juices under her tapping heels."

York straightened in his chair and set down his glass of brandy as a thought struck him. Perhaps there *was* a reason why he couldn't forget the alluring dancer.

Why hadn't he thought of that before? He had already imagined his spring line in terms of Gypsy fire and color, and in his mind Shanda embodied all that a Gypsy was—and more. He would infuse her spirit into his designs.

"Hellyn, you're a sweetheart. You've given me an incredible idea, and I've got to run."

"But York—"

"Talk to me tomorrow," he urged. "I've got to go."

He replaced the phone before she could say anything else. He didn't want to waste a moment. A flood of ideas began to spill into his mind, and he picked up his pencil. Sketching feverishly, he saw the costumes he wanted in vivid detail—each designed with Shanda in mind.

The ideas kept coming, and forgetting all about

sleep, he worked frantically though the night. His mind hot with whirling colors and silky textures, he sketched and resketched outfit after outfit, then went back and altered them over and over again.

The sun was coming up when he finally leaned back in his chair, exhausted. Running a tired hand over the heavy stubble of his black beard, he yawned. For the first time in two days he had gotten the Gypsy out of his head. He had done it by putting her beauty down on paper.

The sketches were quite incomplete, of course, but they were good. He sensed it. Now all he needed was to persuade his Gypsy inspiration to help him when the clothes were ready to model. He would begin tomorrow. If he could convince her to model the white silk in his fall line next month, then he felt sure that she would agree to do his Gypsy spring line as well.

Yawning again, he went to the kitchen for a glass of milk. Then he went to his bedroom, stripped off his clothes, and crawled into bed. He smiled to himself. He was wiped out, but it was a good feeling. He felt triumphant, exuberant. He knew his spring line would be exceptional—just like Shanda, the mysterious Gypsy dancer who had inspired it.

When Shanda awakened the next morning, her first thoughts were of York. *"Aye, aye, aye,"* she muttered, annoyed with herself. Brushing the masses of wavy hair away from her face, she searched for her slippers, then pulled on her robe and made her way across the room to the bathroom.

After she had attended to her morning toilette, she

stumbled sleepily to the kitchen and made a fresh cup of coffee. While it brewed, she fixed a breakfast of fruit and freshly baked bread.

Restless and eager to perform her daily ritual, she finished her meal and dressed in her usual skirt, peasant blouse, and comfortable shoes. Then she colored her lips bright red. Satisfied, she put her few personal belongings and an apple in the huge pockets of her skirt and left the house.

"Hello, Shanda," one of the neighbors called out as she passed. "Are you going to observe the *dilo gajé* again today?"

The dancer nodded, laughing. It wasn't exactly a lie. Each day she went into the teeming city streets and roamed until she grew tired. And everywhere she went, she watched the people she came into contact with.

"Aren't you scared to go to all those strange places?" the woman asked, frowning.

Shanda shook her head. "What's to fear? My fate is predetermined and I must go where my feet take me."

The other Gypsy laughed. "Ah, Shanda, your Gypsy blood is so pure that I envy you." She pointed to the porch she had been sweeping. "Some of us are getting as bad as the *gajé* who live in these boxes, but not you. You are like the wind," she said with a wistful sigh. "You go where you want, and no one can hold you in one place. No *rom*, no father, no mother-in-law, no babies."

Shanda shivered at the thought of all those shackles. "Much success in your *dukkering* today, Blanca. *BáXt.*" Then she strolled away, once more

75

reminded of how fortunate she was. The morning was hers. The day was hers. The world was hers.

Today she was taking the subway to one of the more exclusive sections of the sprawling city. She pushed aside the notion that she had chosen that area because she imagined it would be the kind of place in which York would live.

Emerging from the subway in the unfamiliar neighborhood, she walked among the bustling strangers, unafraid as she studied her strange surroundings. Not caring that she was soon lost, she kept walking until she came to a park. When she was ready to go home, she would find her way.

She was drawn to the children playing uninhibitedly on grassy strips bound by curving sidewalks. She took the apple from her pocket and began to eat her lunch as she watched the freedom of the children's movements. They were the *gajé* most like Gypsies, for they were too young to be controlled by their possessions. They still laughed and danced and lived with the abandon of youth. They had no fears as they set their spirits free on the sweet spring grass and frolicked happily.

Shanda stored the pictures in her mind. She wanted new steps to incorporate into her performances in California, and the children inspired her. She stayed long after they had gone, soaking up the city atmosphere and enjoying the passing parade of people. At last she made her way home so that she could get ready for her performance.

No matter how she tried to shove thoughts of York from her mind, she wondered if he would show up at the club tonight. Or would he honor her request?

76

The question mattered more than she wanted to admit.

York had shopped all day for just the right present for Shanda, but he couldn't seem to find what he wanted. At last he settled for a belt from his own line.

Made of three strands of fourteen-caret gold chains in graduated lengths, it had a richness that might appeal to the Gypsy. He had noticed that she wore some jewelry, and he wanted to compliment her beauty. He thought the belt would do it. In his mind's eye he could see the way the chains would accent her slender waist and full hips as she danced.

"Yes," he said aloud. "Yes, this is sure to please her."

Shanda was back in her apartment by dinnertime, and when the doorbell rang, she tensed. York had been in her mind all day, and she suspected that it was he at the door.

Silently slipping across the room, she thanked God that Gypsies kept their curtains closed at all times to keep the angel of death from peeping in and catching them unawares. The practice also allowed her to see whoever came to her door before they saw her.

To her surprise, she saw York's chauffeur standing on the step, nervously fiddling with a long, slender package in his hand. He kept glancing at the other houses on the street, and Shanda knew that he was acutely uncomfortable in her neighborhood.

A smile on her lips, she opened the door. "Yes?"

"A package from Mr. Summerfield," he announced. When he had thrust it at her, he turned away without another word.

A gift from York. A slight anticipatory shiver raced through Shanda before she could control it. But she made herself muster some disdain. First the flowers and kisses, and now a gift. He was still trying to buy her, trying to use his money to impress her.

Of course, she thought, she would return the gift. But curiosity got the best of her. What could it hurt if she just peeked inside to see what the fashion designer had sent?

She shut the door and hurried over to her bed. For a long moment she stared at the package, then, with the greatest care, she unwrapped the beautiful silver-on-gold colored paper.

When she first saw the chains nestled so exquisitely on the sheer white tissue paper, she sucked in her breath. There were three strands of gold. They were rich and thin and lovely, and if she should wear them all around her neck at one time, they would reflect the light when she danced.

Mesmerized by the shimmering strands, she lifted the chains from the box. Her eyes widened when she saw that they weren't necklaces at all. Her mouth tightened as she held the belt away from her and let the glittering gold strands slip through her fingers until she held only the heavy medallion clasp.

"Aye, aye, aye," she muttered incredulously. She had thought York had given her jewelry, and instead he had given her a gift symbolic of restraint, of possession. Not only had he meant to influence her with his wealth, he clearly intended to show her that he meant to control her.

"A belt!" she cried indignantly. "And of chains yet! The *gajó* fool means to chain me. He thinks to weigh

78

me down with his gold. Baa!" she exclaimed, tossing the gift from her. Bitterly disappointed, she stalked across the room to the small round mirror on the wall. It served her right for accepting the *gajé* gift in the first place. She would know better next time!

"York Summerfield is *prikáza!*" she told the image in the mirror. "Bad luck! Stay away from him!"

But even as she commanded her reflection to obey, her eyes strayed to the shiny chains now cast aside on her bed. Rich and glimmering, the bright gold beckoned.

It was much like the *gajó* stranger who had given it to her, she mused. She just hoped she could cast him from her as easily as she had the chains.

CHAPTER SIX

High up in his penthouse apartment with a view that seemed to reflect much of the civilized world, York stared out his windows as night closed in on the city. His thoughts were not on the scene before him. He could have been anywhere, for his mind was focused on a single woman. Shanda would be dancing soon. He ached to see her, but he was wise enough to humor her expressed desire not to see him until Saturday night.

He drew in a deep breath and exhaled wearily. He had been working hour after hour on his spring line, for work was the only way he could force himself not to go to the club. He turned back to the garment he had been sketching. For a moment he studied it.

His concentration was weak and his thoughts strayed to the belt he had sent the Gypsy beauty. He wondered how she had reacted. He reached for the phone, then remembered that he had no number where he could contact her. Surely that was for the best. He would let her come to him in her own time.

As he gazed at the sketch, his mind slowly began to focus on work. He realized that he had visualized the outfit with the belt of chains, but that had been a winter feature and he never duplicated anything in a later line. His mind on the chains, he began to sketch layers of them over the bodice of the colorful blouse until he had three thin necklaces.

"Yes, that's it!" he cried triumphantly, then bent farther down over the sketch, lost once more in his work.

Shanda was running late when she arrived at the club with Vagan and Miguel. She had dallied when she dressed, the memory of York and his gift weighing on her mind. No matter what she told herself, she couldn't seem to stop thinking about the fashion designer.

She had seen the reflection of the thin gold chains out of the corner of her eye when she peered into the mirror to do her makeup. She told herself that she had only disdain for the designer and his gift, but it did seem a shame to return the chains which shimmered with such golden beauty. Yet she would *never* wear the belt. The mere idea was abhorrent!

Not until the music began and she was able to lose herself in it, did she think about something else besides York and the strands of gold. Once on the stage, she finally gave herself up to the beat which soon put fire in her feet and a flame in her heart.

And still, when she spun and whirled, trying to

escape the designer's image, she looked into each of the *gajé* men's faces to see if she found York's there.

But she did not find it, and she realized that she was disappointed. The evening wore on until she had danced her last dance, and still York did not come.

It was true that she had told him to stay away, but now she was angry because he had obeyed. Did she not haunt his thoughts as he did hers? Did she not linger in his mind like a fire that refused to be put out?

"Baa!" she muttered sourly as she left the stage to resounding applause.

Vagan touched her arm, causing her to turn to him with wide eyes. When she realized it was the Gypsy musician and not York, she frowned.

"What's wrong?" he asked. "You danced superbly."

Of course she would not let him know why she was so unhappy. "My concentration was off. I gave less than my best performance," she admitted, because it was true. "I cheated the audience."

Vagan laughed. "They don't know it, so who cares?"

"I do. Excuse me," she said, pushing open the door to her dressing room. Vagan was smart enough not to pursue her in her present state of mind, and brooding, he went into his own dressing room.

Moments later Shanda heard a knock on hers. She couldn't still the rapid beating of her heart as she made herself calmly walk to her door. When she pulled it open, she found York's chauffeur standing there, holding another box and looking more nervous than he had at the house.

"Mr. Summerfield sent this," he murmured, glancing over his shoulder at Vagan, who posed threateningly in the doorway of his dressing room.

"Take it back to him!" Shanda ordered imperiously. "I don't want it!"

The man didn't seem to hear. He had already turned his back to the dancer and was quickly vanishing down the hall. It was as though all his concentration had been devoted to the task, and when he had performed it, he was no longer involved.

"Mister— Chauffeur—"

Her words were in vain; clearly he had no intention of returning. Her gaze met Vagan's, and she looked at him briefly before reaching down for the present York had sent.

When she had closed the door on Vagan's sullen stare, she tossed the gift on the vanity table. When— if—York came on Saturday, she would return it. She would let him know that she could not be enticed with what his money could buy. She would not admit, even to herself, that she had been excited when the first gift had arrived.

After all, she had not considered what York was trying to do then. A picture of the glistening gold chains of the belt rose in her mind, and she vowed that she would put it back in its box and give it to York.

The week passed with a series of daily gifts which Shanda refused, but the chauffeur left them at her door anyway. Although she was very curious by nature, she had not opened any of them. Ignoring the pretty paper and odd-shaped boxes, she had put the presents aside to be returned to York.

She had not wanted his gifts, but she could not deny that her heart beat a little faster at the thought of seeing him as she waited backstage on Saturday night. Although she had made herself concentrate all week on the dances she would perform in California, persistent thoughts of York had made her more restless than her Gypsy spirit.

When the music began for Saturday night's performance, York was sitting at the same table he and Hellyn had shared a week ago. As he waited alone for Shanda to perform, he experienced a raw sense of expectation and excitement.

He was aware that the Gypsy hadn't seemed pleased when his chauffeur had delivered the gifts that he'd selected so carefully for her. All week long the dancer had tormented him. He had tried to keep preoccupied with his work, but since each design was based on her, she had lived in his mind as though she were by his side.

The lights dimmed and the music started. York gazed at the black curtain as though his life depended upon it. And suddenly she was there—more real, more beautiful, more enchanting than he had remembered. He sighed in relief, but his anxiety didn't dissipate, for now he wanted her more than ever.

Barefoot, dressed in a layered white dress, Shanda burst onto the stage with astounding energy. She spun across the floor from one side to the other, moving so rapidly that it seemed she couldn't possibly focus on any single object.

But she had seen York.

As York viewed the dancer, his heart began to beat madly. To his dismay, she seemed determined to ignore him. But that didn't dim his fascination in the slightest. As he watched her, he could remember with delicious detail how her magnificent body had felt in his arms, how her lips had felt against his, how his body had warmed to her slightest touch.

It was truly as if she had cast some magical spell over him. He told himself that it was just the mystery of her that drew him, but he knew it wasn't that simple.

And what if she rebuffed him tonight? What would he do? He wanted this woman in a way he had never wanted a woman before.

Shanda could feel herself burn under the heat of York's gaze. She was acutely aware that he was sitting at the front middle table, yet she was determined to ignore him, to enjoy him on her terms, at her choosing.

Even though she diligently avoided looking directly at him, she felt as if she were dancing for him alone. Every movement, every step, every gesture was for him. She wanted him to find her appealing, as she had never wanted any other man to.

She knew that she was dancing extremely well, and although it was for the *gajó* stranger, the audience wasn't being cheated this time. At last the final number ended, and she went to center stage and bowed.

She wanted to keep York in suspense tonight, but once she stepped before him, there was no way she could avoid looking into his face. Their gazes locked for a moment, and then York gave her a slow, sweet smile.

Shanda felt as if she had been touched by him. It took great strength to look away and turn to the rest of the audience. Even then she saw the dark hair, dancing eyes, and slow, lazy smile of York Summerfield.

Finally, she calmly and coolly walked across the stage and turned toward her dressing room.

"Good evening."

Her pulse raced when she stepped out into the hall and found York standing in front of her. His dark eyes were smiling at her, luring her with their velvety richness, and she was shocked at the depths of her own response as she stood face to face with him.

"Good evening." There was nothing in her voice to betray the excitement, the exhilaration she felt at standing inches from him.

"It's Saturday," he said, as if she needed reminding.

"Yes, it is," she replied, looking into his eyes. She waited to see what else he would say, but he seemed to expect her to speak. The noise of applause was almost deafening, and Shanda wasn't surprised when Vagan and Miguel appeared behind her.

"Let's take another bow," Miguel told her. "This is the best response we've had yet."

She flashed York a quick look, then let Vagan and

Miguel each take her hand. Vagan clasped her fingers with almost cruel tightness as she ran with the two musicians back on stage, and she did her best to ignore the hostility she sensed in him. They took a second, then a third bow, and Shanda broke free.

Vagan followed close on her heels, and once behind the curtain, he called her name sharply.

"Shanda!"

She spun around halfheartedly, wanting to avoid another blowup with him.

"Stay away from that *gajó* man!" he muttered contemptuously. "Are you going to let him defile you with his touch?"

"Leave me alone, Vagan," she commanded, spinning on her heel so that she could escape.

Her steps slowed as she went to her dressing room. She wasn't surprised to find York waiting there for her. He was smiling and relaxed as he leaned casually against her dressing table, his arms crossed.

Shanda found herself thinking how arrogant he was in his assurance that he could wait in her dressing room. She realized that his pride and confidence matched her own, and she again told herself to be wary of this man.

"Hello again," he said warmly. "I hope you don't mind my barging in like this. I wanted to make sure that I didn't lose you."

The sight of him standing there so boldly, a chocolate-colored shirt setting off his dark looks, his lean hips and long legs encased in beige slacks, made her heart beat faster.

She shrugged casually, hoping to hide both her

agitation and excitement. "It doesn't matter. You've been in my dressing room before."

"I remember that night," he said in a low voice.

Shanda turned away before he could see the gleam in her eyes. Reaching down, she began to take off the slippers she had worn for her final number.

In seconds York was kneeling in front of her. "Let me help you," he said, sliding the soft shoe from her slender foot.

Automatically Shanda balanced herself with her hand on his shoulder. She felt the electricity shoot up her arm with the contact, and she tried her best to devote herself to the task at hand, watching while York slid off first one shoe, then the other.

His fingers lingered lightly on her trim ankle, and Shanda was sure she felt them burn into her flesh, even though York was barely touching her. Her hair had fallen toward her face, and as she looked into his bright eyes, he reached up and entwined his fingers in the ebony waves cascading over her shoulders. Gently he drew her down to where he sat on the carpeted floor.

"I've missed you this week," he whispered thickly. "I could hardly wait until tonight." Then he turned her face toward his and gently caressed her lips.

She could feel the heat of his hard body against hers through the thin fabric of her costume, and she was well aware of the way he excited her. She knew her own body and her capacity to enjoy York's caresses, and she reminded herself that she must keep control over her senses.

When she pulled free of his arms and stood up, he didn't try to stop her. She walked over to her vanity, knowing that she had to get away from him before she was lost to the desire they both shared.

Lifting her chin, she concealed her emotions behind a mask of indifference. "I want to return these," she said as she held out the paper bag full of the gifts he had sent her. She saw the barely discernible narrowing of York's eyes as he gracefully rose from the floor and came toward her.

"Didn't they please you?" he asked, a slight smile on his lips.

"I can't be bought," she told him with a proud lift of her head.

His brows arched ever so slightly. "Forgive me for giving you the wrong impression. I certainly wasn't trying to buy you. You forbade me from seeing you all week, and I only wanted you to know that I was thinking of you. They were given from the heart to please you. I'm sorry if you were insulted."

Shanda glanced at him warily. He sounded all too sincere. She looked at the bag which he had made no move to take and wondered again what was in the boxes.

"Weren't you even curious?" York drawled.

When Shanda saw the big smile on his face, she was sure he had looked inside her head and read her thoughts.

"Yes," she said honestly. "I was curious, but I can't accept these presents."

"All right," he said easily, surprising her. He took the bag from her hand. "Will you go with me to a party tonight?" he asked, still smiling as he dismissed the matter of the gifts.

Shanda didn't know what to make of him. She

couldn't read him at all. He was clever and he knew he had her on the defensive, but he didn't want her to run far enough to escape.

And she didn't want to run that far either, she reminded herself. She hadn't forgotten how eagerly she had looked forward to seeing him tonight.

"What party?"

He shrugged casually. "Just some friends of mine from the fashion world. No one you know, I'm sure, but I think you might enjoy yourself."

He thought the party was a good idea because he could casually introduce her to his world.

Shanda was pensive for a moment. Why not go? she asked herself. What could a few hours matter?

She loved the excitement and challenge of the unfamiliar, and although she had shied away from intimate contact with the outside world, York intrigued her. She was curious to see the world in which he lived. And perhaps, just perhaps, he would lose some of his appeal.

And it would buy her a little more time. She wanted him, and she knew that he wanted her. But she was not ready to succumb to his charm.

"All right," she agreed. "I'll go with you to the party."

CHAPTER SEVEN

York waited while she changed clothes, and once
again Shanda found that she was feeling self-conscious with him. It was a feeling she hated. He was
inhibiting her in a way she couldn't explain.

She gazed at her reflection in the steamy bathroom
mirror, then grabbed up her hairbrush and whirled
away from her image. She was who she was—Shanda
Nicholas, Gypsy dancer—and she had long ago promised that she would live only by her dictates, not any
man's. Her blouse half buttoned, her feet shoeless,
she was tying her full skirt at the waist when she
entered her dressing room.

"The heat in the bathroom," she said offhandedly,
explaining away her state of undress.

"Here, let me help you," York said with a smile,
crossing the room to stand behind her. Not waiting
for her to agree or disagree, he expertly buttoned the
tiny beads that fastened her off-the-shoulder blouse.

She experienced a rush of excitement, but refused

to give in to the shivers running up and down her spine. She made herself concentrate on brushing her hair, but she wondered if he could see the way her fingers trembled.

As she threw the brush down on her vanity, she felt York's fingers in the thick undulating waves moving about her shoulders.

"You have gorgeous hair," he murmured against her ear.

Shanda could feel the erratic beating of her heart, and she turned around to face him before he could stir her senses further. She didn't know what the night would bring. She knew that she wanted to enjoy York, but she would not give more than she wanted him to have.

"Aren't you concerned about being late for the party?" she asked with a brilliant smile. "Don't you people live by the ticking of the clock?"

York smiled at her. "Yes, I'm afraid we do. Don't Gypsies?"

Shanda shook her head. "What does it matter what the clock says? We will live until we die anyway."

York laughed, and abruptly he drew her back to him. "I can't argue with that logic, can I, Gypsy lady?"

"We should go," she said, pulling free. When he was so near, he smothered her with his heady appeal, and she couldn't let that happen.

She wondered if he knew that she was eager to go because of his nearness in the small room. He reached out and lightly caressed her cheek with gentle fingers.

"I don't know if I want to share you with anyone

tonight, Shanda. Perhaps we should go somewhere else—just the two of us."

She averted her eyes. York Summerfield enticed her. The week hadn't given her the time she needed to put distance between her and him after all. She was losing control.

"The party sounds like fun," she insisted, turning away from him. She avoided looking at him while she put on tall, high-heeled sandals. "Let's go."

If he were disappointed, he didn't let her know it. "All right. Whatever suits you."

She could think of other things that would suit her better, but the party was safer.

When they walked down the hall, she saw that the door to Miguel's room was open and he and Vagan were sitting in chairs, talking.

"Shanda," Vagan called out crossly, seeing her with York. "We've been waiting for you."

Tossing back her luxuriant hair in an unconsciously defiant gesture, she said, "Go on without me." With a casualness that belied the tightness in her chest, she announced, "I'm going to a party. I'll be home late."

She could see the storm gather on Vagan's face and she wanted to urge York to hurry, but he stood and waited for some reaction from the two men.

Clearly Miguel wasn't pleased either. "Don't be too late. Tomorrow's a busy day."

Shanda nodded and walked on before Vagan had a chance to speak.

"Why will tomorrow be so busy?" York asked, striding to catch up with her.

"We're rehearsing a new routine." That wasn't a

lie. She only omitted the fact that they would also be packing the car for the trip to California.

Whenever the group, Fever, booked into a club, they insisted that their engagement date not be definite. Because they were Gypsies, they never knew when they would need—or simply desire—to move on.

If management wouldn't agree, they didn't work the club. Tonight they would inform the club manager that they were moving on. Their departure would pose no real problem because there were many groups on standby, waiting for the opportunity to perform.

"I'd love to watch you rehearse," York said with a grin as he took Shanda's arm to lead her to his car. "You've been a great inspiration to me. I've based my entire new spring line of fashions on you."

Her jade eyes widened as she looked at him. She didn't know if she should be flattered or not.

"You can't watch. It's *prikáza*—bad luck."

His dark eyes sparkled and he laughed deeply. "You don't really believe that, do you? Don't you realize that we make our own luck?"

Shanda could feel herself withdraw from him, despite the warmth of his hand. The *gajó* was laughing at her, but *he* was the naive one. The Rom knew things that non-Gypsies weren't privileged to know.

He didn't realize that it was against the good god of life's will to settle in any one place; he clearly didn't know that human beings must ever be on the alert against Arivell, the evil god; or that in the daily constant battle, one needed all the good luck one could summon to fight off the devil.

She and York were worlds apart. He would never understand the Gypsy way in a million years. She had known that from the moment she gazed into his dark eyes. He might have the reckless, burning look of a Gypsy, but there the likeness ended. She had already warned herself that she could enjoy York Summerfield for only a fiery moment, and the flame must die when she moved on. Tomorrow.

She slipped her hand from his and shoved it into her pocket. "I don't let anyone watch me rehearse," she said. "That might ruin the magic."

York laughed again, and Shanda knew that he didn't realize he had upset her. "Nothing could do that, Shanda. You're quite extraordinary. I don't know how anything could possibly dampen your magic."

He looked into her face as the chauffeur opened the door for her, and he touched her shoulder so that she would look back at him. "Tonight I was sure you were dancing for only me. Did every man in the room think the same thing?"

Forcing bright laughter, Shanda slipped away from the caressing warmth of his fingers. "I can't speak for the others—or you. I hope they did. That's the impression I want to give."

Her pulse was pounding at her temples as she slid across the plush softness of the backseat. York could read her all too well it seemed, and the thought made her nervous. She hadn't looked at him throughout the dance, and yet he had known.

"It takes a rare talent to have such an effect on the audience," he mused. "I've seen it only occasionally with my models, but when it happens, it's incredible.

95

It also usually means that girl will shoot right to the top of the fashion world. It could mean riches and success."

Shanda stared out at the New York City streets. She didn't want to think about York and his models.

"Have you ever thought about modeling, Shanda?"

His question caught her unaware, and she turned to him in surprise. "I'm a dancer," she said, as though that answered the question completely.

"Yes, and a splendid one," he said. "But the same qualities that make you so fantastic as a dancer could, I believe, make you a rare and exceptional model."

"Dancing is my destiny," she explained simply. "It fulfills me as nothing else ever could. I have no interest in dressing in *gajé* garments so that someone else can sell store-bought clothes."

York sighed as he settled back against the cushioned seat and gave the chauffeur directions. Shanda wasn't open to the idea of modeling, but it was far from a dead issue.

The penthouse apartment where the party was held was high up on the twenty-first floor, and Shanda was nervous, no matter how much she told herself that she didn't care what the *gajé* fashion world thought of her.

When they were admitted to the apartment by a maid dressed in a frilly black and white uniform, Shanda drew in her breath. She had never in her life seen anything like the apartment.

The living room was three times as large as her entire living quarters, and it was decorated with chrome, glass, and objets d'art. Never had she seen more expensive pieces in one room: paintings, sculpture, vases, books, furniture. And yet it gave the impression of barrenness, of emptiness.

She shivered inwardly as she gazed around the room. So this was the *gajé's* idea of living well. They could have it, she thought. She much preferred the warmth and life of her colorful, crowded room to the false perfection of this cold place.

Her eyes skimmed swiftly over the many people milling about in small groups, whispering and talking low. They all seemed to have lost their individuality in their desire to become individuals. Most, even the shortest, appeared tall and thin, regardless of height. Extensively made up, elegantly dressed in the latest fashions, they reminded her of the mannequins she had seen in the exclusive New York store windows.

She shook her head as she glanced from one to another, huddled in their bunches. And so this was the *gajé* idea of a party. Where was the laughter, the gaiety, the music, the dancing?

As she glanced at York, she remembered the first time she had seen him, and how she had thought him different from the other men at the club. She hadn't thought that he could survive in this kind of sterility. She felt smothered by the sameness, unable to breathe.

Suddenly a low buzz of excitement hummed through the room. Shanda studied the guests, trying to discern the cause. She had herself occasionally caused the same kind of electricity when she danced.

It was as if everyone was aware of some extraordinary happening. She looked from one expensively, exotically clad person to another, and she realized that they were looking in her direction. She was acutely aware of how out of place she looked with her full Gypsy skirt, peasant blouse, and flowing hair.

Abruptly the low chatter resumed, and Shanda suddenly understood what had happened. York. York had entered this room full of people and caused the excitement.

He had told her who he was, but she hadn't understood his power, his appeal. Immediately a stately brunette with bluntly cut black hair sauntered over to them.

"York, darling," she murmured in a whispery, husky voice. "How nice of you to come to my little party. I hope you won't find it too boring."

York smiled indulgently as he took the woman's hand. "I always enjoy your parties. You know that, Monique."

He turned to Shanda. "Monique, I'd like you to meet Shanda Nicholas. Shanda, this is Monique VanHoosten. Perhaps you've heard of her. She's a very famous model and now runs a modeling agency."

"Past tense on the model data," the woman added with a half smile. "My day has come and gone."

Shanda nodded politely. "Hello."

She had never heard of the woman, and she felt uncomfortable when Monique quickly assessed her, then glanced at York questioningly. Shanda had seen the condescending look before, and she defiantly met the woman's hard blue eyes. She never should have come here, she thought.

"Shanda is currently dancing at Sophie's Supreme Club," York offered casually.

Shanda didn't miss the sly, knowing look in the other woman's eyes. "Ahh, the Gypsy dancer. Hellyn told me about you."

She gave Shanda another brief glance, then smiled too sweetly. "Well, do make yourself at home." She looked pointedly at York before she turned away. "I hope you'll meet some of my new girls."

"Of course," York said.

He looked at Shanda as he took her elbow to guide her toward a table laden with refreshments, and he couldn't help but compare her to the perfect, lovely women all around him. They seemed lifeless and cold, clones of the current fashion dictates, from their makeup to the hottest new designs.

Shanda, in her peasant clothes, with her dark hair streaming loosely down her back, put the famous designers and models and ladies of high fashion to shame. Shanda had a glow, a life and that couldn't be diminished by her simple attire.

Now Shanda was aware of another buzz of excitement, and she knew that she was the object of attention. Monique had passed on the news of her identity and it was causing quite a stir in the haute couture circle.

"A *Gypsy*," one woman muttered audibly as Shanda and York passed. "York must be bringing her along for the shock value."

Shanda's only embarrassment came from the slight tightening of York's fingers on her skin. She knew that he, too, had heard the comment. She didn't need

99

his concern. She had heard all the remarks before. She could take care of herself.

She looked directly at the woman who had spoken. "Yes, I'm a Gypsy," she said, her eyes glittering. "How kind of you to notice."

York smiled at Shanda's comment. He understood at once that she was above all this chilly perfection. It was her vigor and vitality that made her so rare and special, and he was even more determined to have her model his designs. She *would* add shock value; she would be amazing.

He turned to the woman and pinned her with his dark eyes. "Yes, her beauty is exceptional, isn't it?"

He was smiling when he faced Shanda, but she didn't miss the brittle glitter in his dark eyes. "Champagne?" he asked, lifting two glasses from the table.

She forced a smile to her lips, then took the glass with a long, elegant hand. Her back rigidly straight, she tossed her rich hair over her shoulder with a haughty motion of her head. Her eyes met York's, and she didn't look away.

"Are you aware that you're the most gorgeous woman in this room?" he asked, holding her gaze.

Before either of them could speak again, a tall, thin girl barely out of her teens came up to them.

"Mr. Summerfield, how charmed I am to meet you," she gushed. She held out a bony hand. "I'm Swan."

"Hello," he said distractedly.

"I've been dying for this opportunity to talk to you," Swan exclaimed. "Is there a chance that you still need someone for your fall line? I've heard that you haven't yet decided on a model for your top number."

"That's rumor," he corrected. "I have decided, but I'll let your agency know if I change my mind. You're with Monique, aren't you?"

She nodded. "I do hope you'll change your mind. Everyone—but everyone—wants to model for York Summerfield."

When York only smiled briefly, Swan lingered a moment, hope clearly shining in her eyes, then wandered away.

Abruptly York tilted his glass to his lips and drank the contents. He didn't know why he thought he had wanted to bring Shanda here. He wasn't in the mood for what inevitably came as part and parcel of these industry parties.

He had been furious at the insulting comment directed at Shanda. The woman would see why he had brought the Gypsy when Shanda modeled his top number in his fall collection and set the fashion world spinning. He didn't need these people, and surely Shanda didn't.

"I'm ready when you are," he murmured. "This was a mistake. I'd prefer an evening with just you and me."

Shanda told herself that he had read her mind. She didn't want to be here either.

Smiling and shaking his head at the people urging him to stay, York guided Shanda out of the apartment to an elevator. In the small space, she was once again aware of how intoxicating York Summerfield was, and she couldn't wait to get outside where there was breathing room. Tonight *had* been a mistake—one she wouldn't make again.

To her surprise, he pushed the button for the thirtieth floor. When the elevator stopped and he motioned for her to exit before him, she frowned.

"Why are we getting out here?"

His smile was slow and lazy. "I live on this floor. I want you to see my sketches."

Shanda shook her head. "I don't think so. As you said, tonight was a mistake. I'd better go on home."

Now it was York's turn to frown. "I did not say *tonight* was a mistake—only the party." He wrapped his arms around her waist and drew her to him before Shanda could protest.

"You aren't escaping so easily, my Gypsy lady. I've waited all week for this night, and I have no intention of letting you run away." He dipped his head and his lips teased hers.

Someone cleared his throat and York drew away from Shanda to glance back over his shoulder.

"Excuse me," a dapper gray-haired man said stiffly, "but are you going up or down?"

York laughed softly. "Out, thank you." Then he took Shanda's hand and walked across the hall.

"Surely you aren't afraid to come in, are you?" he challenged.

"Not at all," she returned automatically.

She wasn't afraid, she assured herself heedlessly. She had seen how York's *gajé* friends lived. Now she would see how he lived. It would serve to further remind that his appeal was purely physical.

And she did want to see his sketches; she was curious to see if he made the lifeless clothes the models at the party had worn. She was almost arrogant in her belief that York and his home would prove a disappointment to her.

And it really didn't matter anyway. After all, she would be gone tomorrow as sure as the sun rose and set. Boldly, she stepped into York Summerfield's home.

CHAPTER EIGHT

Shanda wasn't surprised to find that York's apartment was even more plush than Monique's. But his was rich in a different way—a way that, oddly enough, appealed to her. The plushness cushioned, rather than isolated. The furnishings were expensive, but warm and intimate. There was room to breathe among the beauty and color of the things that contributed to his living space.

She stared around in fascination. To her pleasure, she found that he had a view of Central Park, and she was drawn to the sliding glass door across the room.

York followed her and opened the door so that she could step out onto the balcony filled with greenery and tall trees in mammoth buckets. Soft gold light outlined the vegetation and emphasized its lushness.

"How incredible to find earth and trees up here in the sky," she said. She remembered how she had strolled about the city and wondered where York lived. She had suspected that he would live in one of the exclusive high-rises, but she hadn't anticipated so much natural beauty in the stone and concrete sky-scrapers.

Below them the park lights twinkled, and Shanda went to look over the railing. "It's like magic," she murmured.

She turned when York stepped up behind her and slipped his arms around her waist, drawing her back against him. "So are you," he whispered huskily. With a gentle caress, he brushed her hair aside, and she felt the warmth of his lips on her neck as he spilled kisses over her sensitive skin.

York's provocative touch caused Shanda to shiver, and she knew she must go back inside where the lights were bright and the atmosphere less condu-cive to seduction. But he burned enticingly against her, and already the fire was igniting in her veins.

She could smell the sweet fragrance of the flower-ing gardenias which surrounded them and she found the softly lit, scented balcony garden and the dark, attractive man much too intoxicating.

When York turned her around so that he could kiss her, Shanda let herself be drawn against his hard chest. Her arms slipped around his neck and she met the passion in his possessive lips. The desire that raced through her was so hot that she was alarmed by it.

Her careless assumption that she could handle York on his home ground didn't seem very wise now. She knew how much she wanted him, but she couldn't seem to take the last barrier down. She sensed the danger in giving in to her hunger for him.

105

"I think I should see those sketches now," she said, trembling as she drew away from him.

Clearly the sketches were the last thing on York's mind, but as he watched the Gypsy beauty in the garden light, he forced himself not to think about the aching desire inside him. He had promised himself that he would have this woman. But he had also agreed that he would go at her pace.

"Ahh, the sketches," he murmured, his voice thick with unsatisfied passion. "I did promise to show them to you."

He opened the door again and waited for her to step back inside, and he couldn't stop the rush of desire that spiraled through him. He wasn't used to being denied what he wanted, but he was positive the wait would be worth it.

"In here," he said, leading her to another room.

This one, too, had a view of Central Park, but the room itself was more captivating than the park. Alive with realistic paintings, swatches of cloth of all textures and colors fanning out in decorative half circles, and books of all kinds, the room was surely a fashion designer's dream. But what caught Shanda's attention most of all were the tapestries that hung in varying lengths on one wall.

Lured by their beauty, she crossed the room to stand before one that was hauntingly similar to hers. Men and women in brilliant costumes danced around a campfire. One woman stood out from all the rest, and with her black hair and bright eyes, she was compelling.

"That tapestry is the newest one in my collection," York admitted. "I confess that I purchased it because it reminds me of you. I've found it very inspiring for my sketches."

The mention of his sketches drew Shanda's attention, and after lightly tracing her fingers over the tapestry, she joined York at a long desk.

When he turned the designs around so that she could see them, Shanda sucked in her breath. "They are wonderful!" she exclaimed.

She was thoughtful for a moment as she moved from one design to the next, studying the clothes. "Perhaps you might have pockets on this one," she suggested, pointing to an especially full skirt. "Gypsies love pockets, and some carry any and all their possessions, except their jewelry, in them."

"Thank you for the suggestion," York said, immediately making a note on the sketch.

When Shanda turned to the next sketch, her heart began to beat erratically. The garments were fascinating, but what really held her attention was the necklace that fell across the blouse in three graduated lengths. It was almost as if York had seen into her mind, she told herself, and made the necklace she had expected when the belt arrived.

Saying nothing, she quickly turned to the next sketch. As she looked at each one, she couldn't help but be amazed by York's talent. Because she made her own dance costumes, she had become something of a designer herself, and she saw that York's creations were innovative, yet excitingly authentic and accurate.

The thought frightened her. She had come here expecting to see the smart, tailored, lifeless creations she had seen worn on the thin women at the party.

And she had found incredible warmth and beauty and life in the designs. It was as though York had somehow reached out and grasped the intangible in his hand and held it until he could put it on paper.

"It's as if you have seen into the Gypsy soul," she whispered almost reverently. She was filled with awe when she looked into his eyes. "How did you manage this?"

York smiled. "After I saw you dance, I couldn't get you out of my mind. That night I conceived the idea for my spring line. You kept spinning around and around in my head and I remembered your fire and your excitement. I tried my best to capture you on paper, to infuse your spirit into these designs."

Shanda gasped when his words echoed her thoughts. Anxiously she glanced back at the sketches to see if he had succeeded. It would be a bad thing. She was very superstitious, and she had always been careful not to let anyone take away any part of her.

Now she saw that the *gajó* stranger had indeed stolen some of her movements, her expressions, some little bits of her, for his designs came complete with the Gypsy woman wearing them. And the woman looked extraordinarily like Shanda. She felt threatened, because he had known her such a short time yet knew her so well. So well that he could hold her on paper.

"This is *prikáza!*" she cried in alarm. "You had no right to take any part of me, much less try to capture my spirit. You must destroy the pictures which look like me."

York realized that her fear was very real, and he drew her into his arms. He saw the burning in her eyes and felt the beating of her heart. His fingers were gentle when he brushed back the long masses of wavy hair and cupped her face.

"I haven't really captured any part of you, Shanda," he assured her, his voice as soft and caressing as a summer wind. "I have only tried to duplicate your beauty and your passionate nature. I can't take any part of you by doing that. I just find you so beautiful that I want to share your beauty with the world. There can be no harm in that, can there?"

She didn't know why she listened to this stranger. He was taboo; but he was also very, very exciting. She had been a fool since she met him. Her pulse raced as she looked into his eyes. She quickly closed them again, needing to shut out the sight of his handsome face, his eyes solemn and concerned. He didn't understand her. He never would.

But then, it didn't matter at the moment. Earlier she had promised herself this one night with him, and now it was at hand. The time was right at last.

His touch was sensitive, his breath whispery soft on her skin, his nearness stirring the Gypsy fire inside her, searing away her doubts and fears. Tomorrow would come all too soon, and she would be gone. She wanted the memory of tonight and this man to take with her.

York was deeply troubled because she had reacted so negatively to his drawings of her. It was the last thing he had anticipated, and he wanted very much to assuage her fears.

"I don't understand you, Shanda," he whispered gently. "But I want to know all about you. You must

109

believe that I will never intentionally do anything to hurt you."

His long fingers moved soothingly through her wavy hair, and Shanda felt the soft, warm touch of his lips on her closed eyelids.

She longed to take his words to her heart. Her life was too different from his to explain. His touch was feathery and teasing, and she let herself concentrate only on that. She wanted to abandon herself to the man before her, to her emotions and the moment.

As York gazed at the trembling dark beauty before him, he wanted to touch her in some very real way. She was a rare and special woman, and he ached to know her more intimately.

He stroked the contours of her face with his fingers, letting them trail down to her long and lovely throat. She was gentling like a wild and proud bird. Automatically he bent his head and lifted a kiss from her lips. When they parted slightly under the pressure of his, he held her more tightly, wanting to draw her completely into his world.

Shanda felt his strength, and she was all too aware of how virile and masculine he was. His body spoke to hers with a language as old as time. She listened to the sweet, seductive message, giving herself totally to York's passionate caresses.

He was rich and powerful. He controlled a fashion empire. He was a world apart from her. But she had been drawn to him from the first night, and she could not go away without knowing him more intimately.

They had right now—this rare and pleasurable moment in time—and she was ready at last to take it. Tomorrow would come, regardless of what she did tonight, and her heart and body would no longer be denied the promise of York's love.

York lifted her up in his arms, his mouth still claiming hers as he walked down the hall to his bedroom. He laid her down as if she were a marvelous treasure, then joined her on the silk sheets of the king-sized bed.

His fingers found the tiny buttons of her blouse, and when the gauzy material parted, he drew in his breath sharply. "You're exquisite," he murmured, his eyes glowing with desire as they feasted on her beauty.

For a long moment he studied her, relishing the sight of such perfection. Gently, with a sensitive touch that made Shanda shiver, he traced the contours of her lovely breasts, his fingers memorizing the shape and texture.

Shanda studied him through half-closed lids, barely daring to breathe as his delicate and wondrous touch stirred sensations deep inside her. With a touch so tender that she hardly felt it, York eased off her blouse while he placed kisses on her shoulders. When his hands had followed the shape of her back down to curve around her slender waist, he lifted her slightly so that he could remove her skirt.

Shanda watched in breathless anticipation as he tucked his thumbs lightly into her silk panties and slipped the wispy garment down the long length of her legs. His hands burned everywhere they touched, and he already seemed to know her body better than she knew it herself.

She trembled in expectation as York's subtle seduction and provocative study caused heat to course through her. Dance had been her life, her self-expression, her joy. She had known the thrill of a performance, and she knew the power of controlling the audience and making them receptive to her, but she had never experienced anything like the preparations York Summerfield was making to love her.

She was blossoming under the warmth of his moist mouth and exploring hands; he was awakening feelings in her that she had long kept suppressed. She had always feared that some man would eventually come along and have a key to the heart of her passion. Now she knew that York was that man.

She wanted to abandon herself totally to the joy of the experience for only this one time. She wanted to savor the pleasure she found with him, and she wanted him to enjoy this time with her.

When he had undressed her, he took off his own clothes. Then he sat down on the edge of the bed beside Shanda and gazed at her naked form.

She could hear the mad beat of her heart, and her breathing became harsher as she dared to look at the intoxicating man who so boldly enjoyed her nakedness.

Her gaze slipped over the breadth of his muscled shoulders, and she followed the dark curling hair as it trailed down his lean belly. York was potent and masculine and appealing. She couldn't look away from him, and she couldn't help but think the gods shouldn't have made one man so handsome.

As though he were thinking the same thing about her, York whispered hoarsely, "You're so perfect that you must be a vision, Gypsy woman."

He cupped her face in his hands and lightly lifted a

kiss from her quivering mouth. Then he let his fingertips trail down her throat and over the curves of her breasts. Her nipples became instantly taut as York touched them with a teasing caress, then left them.

He let his hands know the shape of her hips, the sleekness of her abdomen, the length of her legs, and when he began to work his way back up, Shanda trembled.

She moaned softly when he kissed the sensitive insides of her thighs and teased the secret places of her body. She wanted to remember that York Summerfield had tried to steal some of her, but all she could think about was how much she wanted to give now.

Although she had sensed that the union would be explosive, she hadn't anticipated the hunger, the ache that accompanied the desire. Every kiss, every caress, every stroke of York's fingers left her crying for more. She wanted this man with a fierceness that frightened her, but she would not turn back now.

Reaching out, she explored the powerful lines of his body, relishing the feel of his defined muscles and warm skin beneath her fingertips. She tasted him with her lips and licked him with her moist tongue, enjoying the faintly musky scent of him.

"Aye, aye, aye," she whispered at last. "Enough of the dance."

She couldn't wait any longer to know him. The yearning was too intense, the need too great. She wanted to feel his heat against her own. She drew him to her, and when he stretched his long, provocative body over hers, she arched to him erotically.

Carried away on wings of desire, she gave herself up to the touch of his skin against hers, the wild beating of his heart echoing her own, the fierce fire of his mouth and hands exploring her body. Passion rose in her, enfolding her in its sweet strength, making her aware of nothing but this moment and this man who drove her mad with his heady nearness.

As York followed the shapely outline of Shanda's curves with his fingertips and hands, he felt as though he had lost his way in the world and she was his only salvation. He was sure he couldn't breathe, think, function, until he had known the secrets and pleasures of this woman who had danced and spun so tormentingly in his head all week.

"Shanda, Shanda," he whispered thickly as she opened up to him. He had known many women, but this felt like the first time he had ever really made love. The Gypsy caught him up in some kind of emotional fire storm, enhanced by the physical beauty of her loving.

Her touch excited him; her fire ignited his own. She was passionate and uncontrolled, yet her every movement seemed designed to heighten his pleasure. York wanted to lose himself deeper and deeper in her love.

As he moved against her, his every desire was deliciously satisfied. Shanda drew him into a passionate vortex where there were only the two of them, only this shimmering moment.

Just when the flames threatened to engulf them, Shanda cried out some Gypsy word, some ancient expression of total ecstasy.

York had never heard it before, but as he drove into her warmth a last time, he knew precisely what she was saying. He knew that the two of them had touched in the same world for the first time.

CHAPTER NINE

For a long while after their passion had peaked, York rested his weight lightly against Shanda, afraid that if he let her go, she would vanish forever. He could never let that happen. He had found something in her that he couldn't explain, but he knew it played some part in his destiny.

She was a Gypsy vagabond, but if she left, she would take some vital part of him with her. He knew that he wanted her to stay this night with him. And he knew that he wanted her much longer than that.

"You're the most fascinating creature I've ever known," he admitted in a husky voice. "I almost can't believe that I've found you."

Sated from his skilled loving, Shanda lay beneath York in drowsy contentment, listening to his pretty words. Her breathing was still a little irregular as she stroked his back, trying to absorb all the wonders and details of him. She wanted to carry away an image as real as the man himself, but she knew it was impossible.

Her jade eyes were glowing in the dim light spilling from the hall when York finally lay down beside her. He kissed her softly once more, then drew her to his side.

"Talk to me, sweet, sweet Shanda," he coaxed softly. "I want to hear all about you. Where do you call home?"

She smiled gently, knowing he wouldn't understand. "Wherever I choose to stay."

York was thoughtful for a moment as he considered a way to subtly introduce her past. He had to know more about her. He wanted to know more. He needed to penetrate the walls she hid behind.

"Where do your parents live?"

Shanda tensed slightly in his arms, and he drew her closer and soothed her fears with his caresses. He sensed that he had touched on a delicate matter.

She looked at him uneasily. She didn't want him to know the particulars of her past.

"My mother moves around a lot," she said evasively.

He tipped her head and kissed her lips. "Like mother, like daughter," he said with deceptive lightness. He didn't want her to shy further away from him.

Shanda smiled, for she supposed it was true. She really didn't know where her mother was, but the woman had a Gypsy spirit.

"How long has it been since you've seen her?" York asked as she relaxed a little in his arms. He knew that he was treading on forbidden ground, but her past was important to him.

"A long time," she said offhandedly. "Many, many years," she added with the faintest hint of wistfulness in her voice.

"Oh?" York murmured innocently, clearly recalling that Charley had said Shanda's mother had been expelled from the tribe.

"How long has it been since you've seen yours?" Shanda asked, turning the tables on him with a quick defensiveness he had come to expect from her.

He laughed to ease the building tension. He didn't want to spoil the magic of the night.

"Three weeks. She lives in New York—that is, when she's not traveling around the world like a Gypsy."

They both smiled.

"I see," Shanda said, thinking that he must have a warm relationship with his mother. "And your father?"

"He's dead, but I tried to see him at least once a week when he was alive. My parents were divorced and he lived in New Jersey."

"I see."

He had hoped his admission of his parents' divorce would be the impetus to have her open up to him a little, but it wasn't.

"And your father?" he pressed.

She lifted her shoulder in a casual gesture. "I saw him three months ago."

"And your mother wasn't with him?"

Glancing at him sharply, Shanda wondered why he was prodding. "What does it matter?" she asked.

118

He laughed huskily as he hugged her to his long, nude body. "I'm just curious to know about the people who created such a beautiful, special daughter," he said. "Is your mother anything like you?"

"My parents parted," she murmured. "I don't see my mother."

"Wouldn't you like to?"

A vision of her red-haired *gaji* mother rose in her mind. Yes, she would like to see her. But her mother had vanished when she was ordered out of the tribe.

Shanda had searched for a long time for her, but without success. She had suspected that her mother had been so bitter and unhappy that she had not wanted to be found by the daughter who reminded her so much of her former life.

Sadness deepened her voice. "Yes."

For the first time York caught a glimpse of Shanda's bitterness and loss, and he was moved by it.

"What was your mother's name before she married?" he asked softly.

Shanda pulled away from him. "It makes no difference," she said, with a toss of her long hair. She didn't like him asking these personal questions. Her past was none of his business. It had nothing to do with them, with this moment.

York gently drew her back to him and stroked her shoulder. "No, it doesn't. I'm just curious about names. Mine is unusual, as is yours. Was hers?"

"There's nothing unusual about Kaye Wilson," she said. In fact, she had run across several of them in her search for her mother.

York grinned. "No, I suppose not."

He didn't say anything else, but he had said

119

enough to dampen Shanda's happiness. Like most Gypsies, she had a predisposition to become brooding and moody when she was unhappy. The mention of her mother had made her very unhappy.

Now she only wanted to slip away and hide in the darkness as the memories of another time flooded through her. She *did* want to see her mother. And she was sorry that York Summerfield had summoned the ghost from her past—the woman who had been lost to her.

York saw the pain in her jade eyes. When he realized that Shanda had totally withdrawn from him this time, he regretted pressing her about her past. He hadn't wanted to tarnish this beautiful night with her.

He wanted to do something to make her smile again, but he didn't know what would please her. He couldn't give her what she seemed to need at the moment. He could only hope to distract her from her unhappiness. But how?

He would show her the gifts, he decided. He truly wanted her to have them, and she had returned them without even looking at them. Perhaps she would be pleased if she saw what he had gotten for her.

"Stay right where you are," he murmured, then slid off the bed and went down the hall.

Shanda leaned on her elbows as she watched him walk away, and she wondered where he was going so soon after loving her.

To her surprise he returned with the bag full of gifts that she had made him take from her dressing room. His tall, naked form beautiful in the gentle

120

light, he joined her again, scattering the presents on the bed with them.

"I selected every gift with the utmost care," he told her, his eyes bright as they met hers. "I envisioned how each one would look on you."

"I don't want them," Shanda insisted as she looked at the man who had so completely loved her moments ago.

She knew that he was trying to recapture what they'd had, and she wanted that too. She hadn't wanted him to see this side of her—this vulnerable, hurt part of her that she kept hidden away. She wanted a distraction as much as he wanted to give her one. But she could not take his material gifts.

"I want to see for myself how they look on you," he murmured. "You won't deny me that, will you? I spent hours searching for something that would be beautiful enough for you."

"You're a pretty man with pretty words," she teased with a lightness she didn't feel. "But I can't accept your pretty presents."

York smiled enticingly. "Just look at them," he coaxed. "What can that hurt?"

Shanda warned herself sharply that she should not even look, but as she gazed into his compelling eyes, she felt her resolve weaken. What could it hurt? He had gone to great trouble to try to please her. She would not keep the gifts, but she would satisfy her curiosity about them.

Folding her legs under her, she sat up in bed so that she could open the presents, and she could not suppress the small shiver of excitement that shot through her as he handed her the last one first.

"I had a very special man work on this every single day this week—just for you," York told her.

In spite of her experience with the belt, or perhaps because of it, she did want to know what else York had chosen for her, and she carefully removed the embossed white paper. "Aye, aye, aye," she murmured low as she lifted the necklace from the long, slender box. Again she had a feeling that York had read her mind, for she vividly recalled thinking how beautiful the chains would be as a necklace. And not only had he already designed what she had envisioned, he had it made just for her.

"Let's just see how it looks," he whispered low, taking the necklace from her hands.

"It doesn't matter," she insisted. "I can't keep it."

"It matters to me," York murmured as he moved behind her on his knees to slip the thin gold around her neck. When he had brushed her hair aside so that he could lock the clasp, he let his fingers lightly trace the outline against her throat.

The necklace was the most beautiful thing Shanda had ever imagined, and when York turned her so that he could see how it looked, she glimpsed her reflection in a tall bureau mirror. The light was such that she was silhouetted, but the chains caught the scant brightness and reflected it in rich rows of gold.

"It's splendid," she murmured involuntarily.

It was tradition for Gypsy women to wear most of the family's fortune on their person. Jewelry was the Gypsy's big concession to material wealth. Shanda had only a few pieces, but as she traced the thin strands of gold, she told herself that she could see why the women were so taken with jewels.

"I want you to keep this," York whispered. "I imagined how it would look on you when I designed it, and it more than lives up to my expectations."

He realized just how badly he did want her to accept it. It was magnificent on her, enhancing her own beauty in just the right manner.

Shanda reached for the chain with both hands, and before she could take it off, York gently kissed her lips. Then he let his fingers glide down her throat caressingly until he touched her hands. He traced her fingers with his own, then drew her hands away from the chain.

"Your neck is long and slender, and the necklace looks lovely," he murmured. He turned her hands over and placed a gentle kiss in each one before he held out another package to her.

She shook her head. "I really can't take these."

"Just a glimpse," he encouraged.

Against her better instincts, she accepted the small box. When she unwrapped it, she found a single, tiny gold chain.

"It's one earring," York told her with a grin. "I sent one on Tuesday and the other on Wednesday."

He held out the other box, and Shanda unwrapped it. When she had the matching pair, York lifted her hair over one shoulder and expertly inserted the chain in her ear by feeling for the pierced area.

"I sometimes do this in the line of work," he murmured, "but I've never enjoyed it so much."

He dropped a kiss on her neck before he handed her the next package.

This time she found a gold chain so thin that it seemed almost invisible.

"I think that will show just a tiny glimmer of gold when you dance," York told her. "It matches the rest of the jewelry."

Before Shanda could say anything, he bent over her so that he could put the jewelry around her ankle. She remembered contemptuously wondering if the second gift from York would be an ankle bracelet, and she immediately reached out to stop him.

But he looked at her, and their gazes locked. His dark eyes seemed to mesmerize her as he began to lightly stroke the curves of her leg. Shanda shivered under the assault on her senses.

She hadn't wanted his gifts. She hadn't meant to take them. But she found the man before her all too magnetic and hypnotic. His fingers were warm on her skin, and his nakedness was stimulating. His body was hard and lean and masculine, and she felt flushed as she studied his outline carved against the backdrop of the hall light.

When he reached for the final gift, she remembered what it was—the belt of chains she hated. "No more," she said firmly. "I can't take your chains."

She *wouldn't* take them. She had let this go too far.

York opened the package himself. "Here, let me show you," he said in a low voice. "I designed this. It's from my winter line. When I imagined you dancing, I thought of how this would reflect the light. Can you envision the sparkle and richness of the gold against your honey-colored skin?"

For a moment Shanda tried to see the gifts through York's eyes, and in that moment he moved up behind her and slipped the belt around her waist.

Shanda felt the heat of his body against hers, and in

her confusion and agitation, she experienced a sudden and swift rush of untamed desire. York's fingers fanned out over her waist as he locked the broad, decorative clasp on her left side.

The chains lay in thin layers across her naked skin, each one longer than the last as they dipped down low on her right side. York drew her back against him as his fingers gently fondled the strands of gold which now so elegantly decorated her body.

"Such a beautiful woman should have beautiful gifts," he murmured against her hair.

The jewelry was beautiful, Shanda admitted to herself. And so was the man who now molded his body so intimately to hers, his fingers spreading out over the sensitive skin of her abdomen, then moving upward in caressing circles until he had cupped both her breasts. The golden chains made a whispery sound as York disturbed them, and Shanda closed her eyes and exhaled raggedly.

She wanted to forget about the disturbing thoughts which had so recently troubled her. All she wanted at the moment was to experience once more York's tantalizing loving.

She lay down and held her arms out to him. And when he moved into them, Shanda let him take her away from the worries of the world. She had only tonight with him, and then it would be over.

Shanda awakened slowly, a smile on her lips. There was an unusual feeling to the room, and her eyes fluttered open. When she saw that York was snuggled up to her body, one muscled leg thrown over the long length of hers, one tanned arm partially around her waist, the smile died on her lips. For a long moment she glanced back over her shoulder to study the handsome man.

His dark eyes closed, long lashes ebony against his cheeks, his black hair tousled, York looked oddly innocent, despite his potent appeal. Shanda couldn't bear to look away. She wanted to soak up the sight of him so that she could remember it in the dark nights on the road.

When she looked down at her own body, she was shocked to find herself all in chains, from her ears to her ankle. "Oh, no," she whispered, as the memories of the previous night came rushing back to her.

She had let York beguile her, control her with his magic. She had behaved very foolishly. She honestly had never meant to accept his gifts, his chains of gold that glittered too brightly in the early morning sun streaming into the wide windows.

York had touched her so intimately, so completely, that she had lost control. She had given in to his wishes, succumbed to his baubles.

Her face suddenly flamed as she recalled just how deeply York had moved her. She had even told him about her mother. She never discussed the woman with anyone, not even Miguel and Vagan.

"Aye, aye, aye," she muttered now. She had never meant to tell the outsider anything about her past. She had made herself vulnerable.

She would not let him into her world any further, she thought. She could never be like him—controlled by time and people and things, rather than by spirit and nature. They'd had their night, and now she must leave and never see York Summerfield again.

Stealthily, gently, she eased his arm away and slid her leg from beneath his. For just a moment she longed to feel the warmth of his weight again. But only for a moment.

In seconds she had dressed and slipped out the bedroom door. She paused, her heart beating fast. She had planned to take nothing with her but sweet memories of York. She had wanted to leave him with only the memory of her.

But she had taken and given more than she wanted. She had to get away before she lost even more of herself to him.

CHAPTER TEN

Shanda stood uncertainly on the street in the sunshine, her heart pounding. She drew in a breath of the early morning air, then let it slip through her lips.

She had taken her night of pleasure with York Summerfield, and it had been too wonderful to regret. Like a fool, she had also taken his gifts. She would wear them now. She wanted to be ever reminded of her weakness so that she wouldn't make such a bad mistake again.

While she searched for a subway to take her home, she ignored a haunting refrain that said she would wear the chains for other reasons too. She didn't want to acknowledge that.

To her chagrin Vagan was sitting out on the front step as she turned the corner to her house. She sighed heavily when she saw him. York's chains of gold glittered brightly in the morning sun, and she knew that Vagan would see them.

Putting a smile on her face, she nodded as she walked toward him. "Good morning."

"You were out all night," he muttered, a dark scowl on his face.

"So?" she flung at him defiantly. "Did you hold a wake for me?"

"You were out with the *gajó* man," he accused darkly. "And look at you!" His angry eyes flashed over the chains which glimmered so rich and beautifully against her skin. "What price did you pay for the *gajé* jewelry?"

Although Shanda felt a rush of guilt color her face, she tossed her hair over one shoulder. "Nothing," she said sharply.

"Nothing," he repeated harshly, stepping in front of her as she tried to unlock her door. He reached out and grabbed the chains around her neck, and before Shanda could stop him, he savagely jerked the thin strands toward him.

They gave beneath the pressure and Shanda felt the chains fall away. In a fit of fury, she struck Vagan full across his face with her open hand.

"*Dilo* Gypsy!" she cried. "Stay out of my personal life. Leave me alone!"

Vagan rubbed his cheek in surprise, then kicked at the crumpled chains at his feet before he muttered an expletive and stormed into his own apartment.

Shanda stared down at the broken necklace. It occurred to her that Vagan had broken one of the chains that had bound her, and though she had resented him for interfering in her life, she knew that he had only done what she could not bring herself to do.

She should just leave the necklace and go inside. But she found that she couldn't do that either. What price *had* she paid for it? she wondered, echoing Vagan's bitter question.

Bending down, she gathered the chains in her hand. The clasp had torn loose on one side, but all the chains were intact. With a scowl as dark as Vagan's, she went into her apartment and set about repairing the necklace.

When York awakened several hours later, he rolled over and eagerly reached for the woman who had fulfilled his greatest desires. When he found only an empty bed, he opened his eyes wide, trying to shake free of the deep sleep that had held him a contented captive for the last few hours.

"Shanda?"

She wasn't in the room. Pulling on a short robe, York stumbled sleepily down the hall and glanced around the living room. She wasn't there either. When he went into his studio, he didn't find her. He searched the apartment for her, but she had vanished as surely as if she had never been there. Only the sweet visions of her remained, once again dancing in his mind.

He ran his hands through his hair as he went back to the bed and stretched out. He could track her down at her house, but he suspected that wasn't the best plan right now. He would wait until tonight and see her at the club.

She needed more time. Their worlds had touched, but his was much too foreign and hostile. He had realized that at the party. He would give her more time—but not much. He was afraid of losing her.

Shanda did not rehearse the California performance with her two partners that day, but she did pack. She was ready to travel by the time she went to the club to dance her final night. Decorated with the thin chains, she sat stonily between Miguel and Vagan as the guitarist drove to the club. If Miguel thought anything at all about her new jewelry, he was too discreet to say so.

Shanda suspected that Vagan had already told him what had happened. His eyes dark and brooding, Vagan stared blindly out the window as Miguel maneuvered the old car through the city streets.

None of them spoke as they readied for the performance, and Shanda was filled with unhappiness as she watched the two musicians walk out onto the stage for the final time. She regretted the angry scene with Vagan, but not as much as she regretted getting involved with York Summerfield. He had brought her bad luck in more ways than one.

She had made a mistake that wouldn't be easy to rectify. She knew that now. York wouldn't be merely a potent memory to be recalled on long Gypsy nights. He had burned into her heart and soul. He had left her aching and confused. She only knew that she had given him some part of her that she could never reclaim.

And what did she have in return? The chains that now bound her body? And the memories that heated her skin and weighed heavily on her heart?

"Baa!" she muttered beneath her breath as she made ready to spring out onto the dance floor.

Sitting at the center table in front of the stage, York's eyes glittered brightly as he watched his exotic Gypsy dancer spin out in front of him. Tonight she seemed more beautiful than ever, and he saw that she wore the chains he had given her. They moved brightly in the colored lights, and he smiled to himself remembering how Shanda had felt beneath his fingertips when he had adorned her with the jewelry.

He was sure she had seen him at the table, but again tonight she danced without looking at him. He wondered if she were embarrassed after their night of love. He couldn't imagine how anything so wonderful could embarrass her.

He gazed at her steadily, willing her to look in his direction. Didn't she realize that they had only just begun? Didn't she know that she couldn't avoid him by not looking at him?

Shanda could feel York's gaze, and she almost couldn't bear it. She was disappointed in herself. She had considered the possibility that he would come tonight. After all, she had run out without a word. But she had told herself that she could ignore him for the two hours she danced.

Now she knew that she had been wrong. She was acutely aware of him sitting there watching her. Her mind filled with memories of the incredible love they had shared, and she felt flushed and faint.

She found it painful to think of never seeing him

again, and yet she knew that she must leave. They had no future, and she didn't dare let him touch her again tonight. She had the memories to take away with her—all she could live with.

The two hours seemed intolerably long, but finally she finished her last dance. As she bowed to the audience, her heart would not let her walk away from York Summerfield without looking at him just one more time.

Her eyes met his, and for a moment she was sure she would drown in their rich depths. And as she saw his slow, lazy smile, she backed away as though he had reached out and touched her. He held a huge bouquet of red roses in his hand, and when he stood up and walked toward her, Shanda vanished behind the black curtain.

Her heart hammering, she rushed down the hall to her room. Not even stopping to change clothes, she picked up her few belongings and headed for the car parked in the back alley.

Weaving his way through the audience, York hurried down the hall to the dancer's dressing room. When he opened the door, he found that she had already gone. He spun on his heel, nearly crashing into Vagan, who stood in the doorway of his room.

"Where is Shanda?" York asked.

"None of your business, *gajó,*" Vagan growled. "Go back to your *gajé* women and forget that you ever coveted one of ours."

Miguel stepped around the violinist. "Come on, Vagan. Let's go," he coaxed, ignoring York. Both musical instruments in hand, he went down the hall.

York started after the guitarist, but to his surprise,

Vagan struck him across the face. The blow was vicious and totally unexpected, and York cursed himself for not being prepared.

His face throbbed with pain, and he turned just in time to block a second blow. When he realized that the Gypsy was holding a heavy club, he knew why his face hurt so fiercely.

A bitter battle ensued between the two men, but York succeeded in kicking the weapon from Vagan's hand. Miguel reappeared to aid the violinist, and though he found that the guitarist wasn't nearly the adversary Vagan was, the two men were tough opponents with a street style of fighting that included its own brand of martial arts.

A well-placed kick caused Miguel to briefly double over with pain, but York's involvement with the guitarist gave Vagan the chance to retrieve his weapon. York received a second blow to the side of his face.

He sank to his knees, stunned by the attack. He was an accomplished fighter, but he had never had occasion to use the skills he had acquired in class. As he heard fleeing footsteps, he cursed himself for not being better prepared to handle a hooligan like Vagan.

"A man could get killed doing this," he muttered to himself as he tried to straighten up.

Shanda climbed out of the car when she saw Vagan and Miguel running toward it.

"What happened?" she asked, alarm in her wide green eyes.

"The manager tried to short our pay," Vagan lied. "We had to use some persuasion."

He glanced at Miguel as though challenging him to

refute the facts, but the blond guitarist didn't say anything.

Miguel's ribs ached, and he wondered if York hadn't cracked one. He had been on the losing end of fights before. He knew that the only thing to be done for a cracked rib was to tape it up. He would do that himself when he was far enough down the road. Right now his primary fear was the police, and he had no intention of waiting for them.

"This place has been nothing but *prikáza*," Shanda muttered unhappily, and she wondered if it all hadn't been her fault. Things had been going well until she got mixed up with York. She had certainly never expected financial trouble with a chic place like Sophie's Supreme Club, but it wasn't the first time Fever had difficulty getting their money.

Her thoughts had been too full of York to worry about her partners, and she felt guilty. Turning to Vagan, she gazed at him anxiously. "Are you hurt?"

His nose was bloody, but he dismissed it. Any pain had been worth beating the *gajó* stranger who had held Shanda's attention.

"I'm all right. Let's get out of here."

Glancing at Miguel, Shanda asked, "Are you okay?"

He nodded. His ribs hurt too much to permit conversation. When he had placed the musical instruments on the backseat, he handed the keys to Vagan.

"You drive," he instructed. Then he ushered Shanda into the front seat and climbed in beside her.

With a grinding of gears and a peeling of tires, Vagan sped away from the dark alley. Shanda glanced back over her shoulder only once, and when she felt the tears fill her eyes, she stared straight ahead.

York could make out the fuzzy image of someone coming down the hall, offering help, but he didn't have time to indulge his wounds. Brushing past the man, he made his way on wobbly legs to the rear exit of the building.

He was just in time to see the backs of Shanda, Miguel, and Vagan's heads as they drove away in an old Buick with California license plates. York strained to make his eyes focus, and he forced himself to remember the identifying numbers and letters on the license.

As the car disappeared into the darkened city streets, he straightened painfully and drew in a deep breath. Then he laughed softly.

"So," he muttered self-mockingly, "Hellyn was almost right. Those damned Gypsies did nearly put my martial arts to rest."

Still, it wasn't the physical pain that hurt so much. He didn't understand what had happened with Shanda. But he intended to find out. He had been sure they had shared something incredibly rare last night. Was he the only one who thought so?

He shook his head in confusion, trying to clear away the cobwebs, and pain shot up the side of his face. He tested his jaw to see if it was broken, then gingerly touched his face below his eye. It felt as if it were on fire.

"Dammit!" he swore sourly. He didn't know what the hell he thought he was doing. His fall show was less than three weeks away, and he would look like the wrong end of a train wreck from the feel of things. His steps less than certain, he made his way to the car.

When the chauffeur saw him, he hurried forward. "Good heavens, Mr. Summerfield. What happened?"

"I've heard somewhere that it's called love," York drawled mockingly.

"Love?" the startled chauffeur repeated. "Did the Gypsy dancer do this to you?"

York couldn't help but break into amused laughter. Shanda had turned him inside out, all right, but she hadn't attacked him. At least not yet.

"No, not the lady. Her male companions. I think the violinist is in love with her, and I believe he called this defending his territory."

He shook his head. Maybe the violinist couldn't be held totally to blame. Shanda was a woman a man could easily love.

He shook his head again. He didn't know what he was thinking. It must have been those damned blows to the head. They had scrambled his brains. His thoughts growing more muddled, he waved aside the chauffeur's ministrations and slid into the car.

"I think," he said pensively, "that we should make the next stop a hospital."

CHAPTER ELEVEN

The trip to California was long and wearying, despite the many friends Shanda and her two companions saw along the way. She was glad when the week ended and they found a new place to live in the busy Los Angeles area. She needed very much to lose herself in her work, for thoughts of York plagued her mind.

The night before her first California performance, she awoke in the darkness, imagining that York was lying by her side. The disappointment of finding herself alone was almost overwhelming. She had honestly thought she felt his presence. She couldn't stop thinking about the way he had touched her, the way he had moved her. And she wondered if he thought of her at all.

She was dressed an hour early for the show that night, and although she assured herself that she was simply suffering opening night jitters, she wasn't positive that was the case. York played on her mind, his brown eyes glowing, his smile sweet and lazy. Everywhere she looked, she saw his face. The vision haunted her. She had run hundreds of miles, but she could not escape.

Clothed in a somber black dress that fitted her mood, her hair pulled back in a tight French bun, her eyes blackened with an eye pencil, Shanda held a rose in her teeth as she made a dramatic entrance on the stage of the elegant nightclub.

The chains she wore constantly to remind her of her mistake with York were her only accessories, and they glittered richly in the light as the dancer propelled herself across the floor from one end of the stage to the other. She concentrated fiercely on the music, and finally, mercifully, her feet found their fire and her heart lifted from the blackness of the loss of York.

Yes, she told herself, this was what she needed. She would belong to no man; she would give her heart solely to the dance and the passion it stirred within her.

With each song, she knew that her performance grew better and better, and by the time she stepped on the stage for her final number—her hair long and flowing, her costume a flaming red two-piece that left the belt of chains to beckon enticingly against her bare skin—she was sure she had succeeded in driving back York's memory. At least for the moment.

Shanda's movements were wild and free as her feet made a rhythmic tapping that matched the rapid beat of the music. She heard vociferous applause and the sound drew her to the front of the stage as she ended her dance with a split that took her all the way to the floor, her head bent, her hair cascading forward. A smile on her lips, she tossed the ebony waves back and looked at the clapping patrons.

Her heart stopped beating. Her eyes blinked. Her smile trembled. She was sure that she was seeing things, sure that she had danced to the point of exhaustion.

York Summerfield was sitting right in front of her, center stage, his eyes hypnotizing, his smile as lazy and easy as ever. Shanda looked more closely, then had to fight to control the gasp that threatened to steal her breath away. He had been injured somehow. His eye was black and there were stitches down the side of his face.

For a moment she was immobilized by his compelling gaze. Miguel and Vagan sounded a refrain, signaling that she should leave the stage, but she didn't know if her feet would carry her.

What had happened to York? What was he doing here? How had he found her? And now that he had, what would she do?

Her limbs as heavy as lead, she somehow managed to get up from her difficult position with some measure of poise and walk off the stage. But she was sure she would die from the heavy pounding of her pulse and the savage beating of her heart.

When she walked toward her dressing room, she wasn't in the least surprised to see that York was also heading there. He didn't say anything and neither did she. She didn't know what to say, what to do.

Abruptly Vagan appeared out of nowhere, a

weapon in his hand. *Gajé* fool!" he muttered. "Did you come for more?"

Shanda sucked in her breath as he approached York, his dark eyes wild and glittering. "Vagan! No!" she cried. "Stop it!"

But it was too late. Vagan swung the club. York ducked, spun on his heel, and landed a well-placed kick against Vagan's back. The musician went down, but quickly scrambled to his feet and rushed York again, the weapon raised.

With one hand York disengaged the weapon, then dropped the musician to his knees again. Shanda pressed herself against the wall of the wide hall and stared in dismay as the two men fought, Vagan panting and crazed, York cool and silent and very, very deliberate in his motions.

When Miguel appeared in the hall, Vagan called for help, but the guitarist only shook his head. "Man, you're on your own. I've only got so many ribs I can afford to have broken," he said solemnly, then turned toward his room.

York waited, willing to stop the madness if the musician would, but Vagan struggled to his knees and swung wildly again.

"Stop it, Vagan!" Shanda pleaded. "Stop it!"

York glanced at the dancer, wondering for whom she was concerned, and Vagan used the moment to swing again, this time connecting with the side of York's face that was stitched. Without any visible sign of anger, York aimed for Vagan's ribs, and in seconds the man was down again, this time for good.

The blood had begun to seep down York's face

from the reopened wound, and Shanda rushed to him without thought.

"You're bleeding," she said urgently as she reached out to touch his cheek.

She heard Vagan groan for the first time, as though he were finally admitting defeat. Shanda's eyes filled with tears as she looked from York to Vagan, doubled over on the floor.

Vagan glowered at her bitterly, then stared at York, his humiliation complete. "Take her, *gajó* fool," he growled. "I wouldn't have her now." With as much dignity as he could muster, he struggled to his feet.

Shanda tried to help him, but he brushed her aside. "Don't touch me," he ordered coldly. "You're unclean!"

Shanda gazed after him as he slowly walked away, his hands clutching his chest.

Blood streaming down his face, York watched with bated breath to see what the Gypsy woman would do, and when she looked back at him with sad green eyes, he sighed.

"Your friend will live," he assured her. "He might hurt a little, but don't we all?"

Shanda shook her head, then, resignation in her steps, she guided him to her dressing room. He had been hurt, and she couldn't turn away from him. Vagan had hurt him the first time, she now knew, and her heart ached because she had been the reason for his pain.

When she motioned for him to sit down, he silently obeyed. He watched as she ran cold water over a cloth, then returned to hold it against his wound.

The nearness of her intoxicated him, and the

throbbing of the injury was soon overshadowed by the pounding of his heart. He ached to hold her in his arms.

"Why did you come here?" she asked bitterly. "How did you find us?" She had hoped she would be able to put the designer and the torrid night of love behind her forever—eventually.

"A private detective traced your license number to your home area, then narrowed down your location by calling surrounding clubs to see if you were booked to dance."

"But why?" she murmured again.

"I was afraid I'd lost you forever," he whispered softly. "Why did you run away like that, without even telling me?"

Shanda's fingers trembled as she tried to press the cold cloth to his handsome face. "I didn't want you to know where I was going," she answered honestly.

"You can't mean that," he insisted in a low, sad voice. He reached out to draw her down on his lap, his fingers touching the gold chains around her bare waist. They needed desperately to talk, but right now he wanted only to hold her, to touch her.

Shanda still thought that she could drive him away. She had to, no matter how difficult it was. She told herself that she would forget him in time. She had her life and he had his.

But as his fingers stroked warmly over her skin and his lips found the curve of her throat, she dropped the cold cloth from her hands. She had always taken what beauty she could find when it was offered, and he was offering something beautiful. He gave her

143

greater pleasure than any man, and her sensual nature would not be denied.

One more time with him couldn't hurt. He had risked a lot for her, and she wanted him too much to send him away. No one, including Vagan, would make the choice for her.

"Your injury," she whispered.

"It will be healed by your love," he said, his breath warm against her skin.

His mouth closed over hers possessively, and Shanda gloried in his hunger. She had missed him in their days apart, and she wanted all that he had to give her now.

When his fingers skillfully untied the knot that held her midriff blouse together, Shanda locked her fingers in his hair and pulled him closer so that she might more fully enjoy the feel of his mouth.

His tongue sought out one taut nipple while his fingers traced the curve of her breast, and Shanda closed her eyes, wanting only to let the sweet sensations blot out her thoughts.

York's seduction was skilled and exhilarating, and soon Shanda forgot all the reasons she had run away from him. She let him sweep her away with him on a tide of love, relishing each wave of ecstasy, each surge of pleasure, each engulfing moment of wild passion as he kissed and caressed her.

When he stood her on her feet and began to unwrap the skirt to her costume, she murmured, "I haven't yet had my shower."

He grinned at her. "I haven't either. I was so afraid that you would escape that I checked into a nearby motel and rushed right down here."

His eyes roving over her hungrily, he let her skirt fall to the floor, then quickly took off his own clothes. "Come with me," he whispered. "We'll turn the water to steam."

Shanda had never taken a shower with a man. It wasn't a correct thing to do in her society, but she felt a shiver of excitement at the idea.

York lightly brushed her mouth with his, then led her to the bath off to one side of the room. One hand still holding Shanda's, he reached into the shower to adjust the water, then he pulled her inside with him.

She was acutely aware of his closeness in the small space, and as the warm spray beat down on them, she smiled. Wet, hairy, and well-defined, York was all too appealing with the cascades of water pouring down his body.

"I'll bathe you first," he whispered, taking a bar of blue soap in hand.

Shanda inhaled sharply as he reached out with his soapy hands and moved them caressingly over her body. Her hair was clinging wetly to her neck and back, and she was sure she had never known a moment quite so intimate when York slid his hands around her waist and up under her hair.

Drawing her to him, he let his tongue trace the dewy outline of her lips, and when they parted beneath his teasing touch, he explored the soft insides of her mouth. Shanda's tongue touched his, and as York toyed with it erotically, a shiver raced up her spine. He held her nearer, and a fire flamed out of control inside her as she felt the power of his desire.

Slowly he let his hands slide down over her back until he cupped her derriere. Shanda drew in her breath sharply as he eased his powerful legs between hers, then gradually filled her with his potent masculinity. She automatically responded as she felt him penetrate deeper and deeper into her velvet depths.

York thrilled to the wonder of her as she caressed him. He began to move against her slowly, deliciously, each moment too precious to rush, each movement too thrilling to hurry.

Shanda moaned softly as the sensations spread throughout her body in waves. She stroked York's back and unconsciously used her supple and skilled dancer's body to make desire exquisite madness, passion a star-studded journey to the heavens.

Time had no meaning; the outside world didn't exist. There was only the two of them and the power of their love.

"Shanda?" York murmured hoarsely.

"Yes," she answered his unasked question. "Yes." And the moment became an entry into a magical sphere. Here in the circle of York's arms, she had found a world for them alone.

In the throes of ecstasy, they clung to each other, listening to the pounding of their hearts in perfect rhythm, the thrumming of love in their veins, the blending of their bodies and souls.

For a long time after love's descent, they held each other, oblivious to the fact that the shower water now ran cold. Shanda wanted this moment to last forever, and York silently promised her that it would.

At last he turned around and shut off the water. "I don't want the tank to run dry," he joked.

He reached for a towel and began to dry Shanda

146

with the most gentle of movements, lovingly rubbing the thick terry over her body and long hair.

She watched him as he worked, and she didn't want to leave the intimacy of their little world here in the shower. When they stepped out, they would have to deal with reality. She lingered even while a smiling York dried himself.

At last he turned to her and lightly touched her lips with his. "I've been told that a man can live off love alone," he murmured, "and while I'm willing to try if you are, I'd also go for a conventional dinner. I haven't eaten since last night. I missed breakfast this morning, managed to miss lunch because I changed planes twice, and then I missed dinner. There's an attractive restaurant near my motel. What do you say?"

The sight of his handsome face marred by the black stitches reminded her of his fight with Vagan. "I can't," she murmured. "You should see a doctor about your wound, and I've got to see how Vagan is. I don't know what will happen to the group now."

York held her chin in one hand and forced her to look at him. "My wound will be fine. Don't worry about me. See about Vagan if you must, but don't run away from me again. Promise me that right now."

She lowered her eyes, knowing that she shouldn't agree, but he tipped her chin back farther.

"Shanda, promise me."

Her green eyes met his penetrating dark one. "I can't make promises when I can't know the future. But I'll stay for a while."

York watched as she quickly dried her long hair

with a high-speed dryer, the waves shining with glossy brilliance as they fell in place.

"I'll meet you here in front of the club in twenty minutes," she said. "I don't want any more trouble with Vagan, so it's best you don't come with me."

He couldn't argue the logic of that, but as he watched her slip out the door without another word, he wondered how far she would go and if he would see her again. She had agreed to return and he had to trust her, but he had a sinking feeling inside. He knew she could easily vanish into a Gypsy community if she wanted to, and no amount of private investigation would uncover her.

When he realized how severe his loss would be, his insides tightened painfully. He couldn't hold her against her wishes, and the thought sobered him. His mind spinning, he went around to the front of the club and stood out on the street to wait.

When Shanda reached Vagan and Miguel's apartment, she rapped twice on the door, then opened it. She was startled to find Vagan packing.

"What are you doing?" she asked, a frown marring her pretty features.

He ignored her, his back to her as he put his few belongings in a knapsack. Miguel sat silently across the room. Shanda turned questioning eyes to him, but received no satisfaction. He only smiled and shrugged.

"Vagan?" She stepped closer as an anxious feeling swept over her. She hadn't realized just how much like a brother he was until now, and she couldn't bear to be shut out by him like this.

Finally he turned to face her, and the anguish she read in his eyes pained her. "Even I must eventually face the truth, Shanda." His eyes were no longer dark and brooding. There was only emptiness and resignation. "I can't change you," he said. "No one can. You'll always be a renegade woman. You'll make no man a wife—certainly not me. I can't tie you to me with anger and threats, and I can't win you with confessions of love. I'm going away before my desire for you eats me alive."

His gaze softened, and for a moment she saw a glimpse of the old Vagan as he caressed her face with his eyes. "You're poison to me—pretty poison—and I can't stand it anymore. I can't watch you spin and whirl and weave your magic for the *gajé* when I want you for myself."

He clenched his fists impotently at his sides. "I thought I could take you back to a true Gypsy way of life, but you've defeated me. I'm the one who must go."

Shanda held her breath as he spoke, but she could feel a blackness spreading inside her. "Where?" she asked, forcing her lips to move.

She had often thought she must break up the group because of Vagan's possessiveness, but now that it was actually happening, she felt a deep sense of loss. Vagan and Miguel had been her only real family for years. She could find other musicians, she realized, but not like them. They were exceptionally gifted, and they knew how to complement each other in their performance.

He shrugged. "Where do Gypsies go?"

Shanda hadn't felt so distraught since she had run

away from home at seventeen. After that she had followed her feet, right along with Vagan and Miguel. They had been her mainstay. But this time she stood all alone. She didn't know where Vagan was going. And he was not going to tell her.

His eyes searched her face once more, but he knew there was no hope. "I need to pack," he said.

Shanda understood that he was dismissing her, that he wanted her to leave him in peace, but she couldn't seem to walk away. She was suddenly bereft. She looked at Miguel, her eyes full of questions.

When he slowly shook his head, she turned toward the door. She had no other choice. It seemed that they both had closed themselves to her.

Out on the street she drew in a steadying breath. She felt as if she had just lost everything she had. She could go on without Vagan and Miguel, but it wouldn't be the same. She spun around when Miguel stepped up behind her.

"He has to go," he said quietly. "You know that, Shanda."

She nodded, but she felt a rush of tears burn her eyes. She did know it, but that didn't ease the loss she felt.

"And you?" she asked. "Have you turned your back on me too?"

He shook his blond head. "No. You can't be rid of me as you can Vagan, but I am going to take some time off until we can find another violinist. I'll probably stay awhile with my *vitsa*. You can reach me there if you want me."

He lightly caressed her cheek as his blue eyes studied her face. "You should take some time off, too,

Shanda. I don't know if you know what you're doing."

She knew that he was talking about York, and she tossed back her hair in a defiant gesture. "I always know what I'm doing," she insisted. But she wasn't as positive as she pretended.

When twenty minutes had come and gone, York began to pace the sidewalk restlessly. He asked himself what he was doing in Los Angeles waiting in front of a nightclub for his Gypsy lover. A single week ago the whole thing would have sounded ludicrous. But now his entire future seemed to revolve around it.

At last he caught sight of Shanda, and he dashed across the street to meet her. "I thought you'd gotten lost," he said with what he hoped was a teasing tone.

Shanda was pleased when she saw him. Suddenly she didn't feel so alone. "I didn't get lost," she said.

"How is Vagan?" he asked.

Shanda looked into his eyes to see if his question was sincere. He had beaten Vagan, and she hadn't expected him to be concerned about the other man.

"He'll be all right," she murmured, and she couldn't hide the unhappiness she felt. "He's going away. Miguel has decided to take some time off, too, until we can find another violinist."

York gazed evenly at her. "What will you do about your commitment here at the club?"

She shrugged with a casualness she didn't feel. "We won't perform here again. The owner won't be pleased, but they always have someone in the wings to fill in vacancies."

"Let's go eat," he suggested. "Food can do wonders for all the world's ills."

Shanda knew that she needed to eat. She was weak with a feeling of loss, and her time with York had drained her. At the moment she really didn't want to be alone. She needed a friend. She met York's eyes, and suddenly she realized that no matter how much her feelings for him frightened her, she did see him as a friend.

"All right," she said.

She didn't know what she would do in the long run, but right now she would have dinner with York. She could return to her tribe for a while too. But at the moment that was the last thing on her mind.

CHAPTER TWELVE

The restaurant York took Shanda to was a pretty Italian place with isolated tables, lots of greenery, and just the right atmosphere.

As they enjoyed a meal of veal parmigiana and wine, York asked, "Will you find another violinist?"

Shanda lowered her eyes and toyed with her napkin. "I don't know." When she met York's eyes, he saw the distress in hers. "I don't know if I can be happy with anyone else. Vagan and Miguel were extraordinary musicians together."

"I'm sorry about the breakup," he said. "I don't want to be responsible for your unhappiness."

Shanda knew that his concern for her was real, and she found herself opening up to him. "You weren't," she said. "You were only the straw that broke the camel's back, as they say. Vagan wanted a relationship I didn't want."

"He *is* in love with you, isn't he?" York asked.

Shanda shrugged. "He only thinks he is."

He smiled. "I can understand how that could happen."

Their eyes held for a moment, and Shanda didn't know what to say. There was an awkward pause, then York spoke again.

"Now that your Vagan is gone and Miguel is taking some time off, will you stay here in California?"

"I'm not sure," she replied, then, because she felt uncomfortable with the question, she turned the tables on him. "Will you return immediately to New York? Don't you have commitments?"

"Yes. I have my fall show in less than three weeks. I'm very excited about it," he said, his eyes suddenly bright. His voice animated, he told her about the event, then he reached across the table and clasped her hand in his. "The highlight of my show is an incredible white dress that's made for you. I knew it the first time I saw you dance."

He still wanted her to model. She had a vibrancy that the other models didn't have, and he sensed the difference her spirit would make to the dress and the modeling of it. Perhaps the time was now right to suggest it. Maybe she could benefit from a little time away from dance.

"Why don't you come back to New York with me?" he said. "You don't have any commitments now."

"No," she returned swiftly, as she removed her hand from his. "That's not for me. I could never stand the confines of modeling."

"Only a single dress," he urged. "There will be nothing confining about it. I'll have it made up in your size and you won't have to rehearse. Just do what comes naturally to you."

154

He wanted her to model his Gypsy line, too, because it had been created for her, but he would not say that now.

Shanda shook her head. "I'm a dancer. I need to create, to express what I feel. I can't live by clocks and clothes. I live for today, for the moment, and I never know what it will bring. I must be free and unrestrained to come and go as I please, to travel or stay, to laugh or cry."

York listened, enthralled yet uneasy, as Shanda described the life she chose to lead. She was fiercely independent, and as he looked into her eyes, he feared that she was slipping away from him again.

They needed to spend some uninterrupted time together, he thought. He had already made arrangements to rent an unoccupied beach house while he sought Shanda.

"I'll be staying at a friend's place in Laguna Beach for a few days. Grab a bathing suit and come with me," he invited. "I think we both need a break from our routines."

Shanda automatically shook her head. "I can't."

"Why not?"

She lowered her gaze. What she really needed to do was spend some time alone, sorting out her situation. She didn't know what she would do, and she had really expected York to return to New York immediately.

"I've just rented a place," she said, as if that explained all the complications she faced.

"No problem," he said smoothly. "I'm only asking you to spend a few days relaxing with me at the beach."

155

"I really can't," she insisted.

"Tell me why."

As she raised her eyes and looked into York's, she was all too aware that she didn't have reasons he would understand. She did need a break herself. But she needed it away from him.

"I don't have a suit," she replied simply. That was the truth, but certainly the least of the reasons why she shouldn't stay with him.

He grinned at her. "No problem. As you well know, this is southern California. The shops haven't closed yet. And this is the place for buying a swimsuit, I'm told."

Shanda smiled slightly at him, and she realized how easily he tempted her. She did want to spend more time with him, and the moment was right. Perhaps, just perhaps, a few days with him would finally satisfy her, and she could at last go away with only memories to treasure, instead of a haunting desire.

"Let's do it," he said boldly, taking her hand to pull her up from her chair. "I have a rented car, and I passed a shopping center en route to the club. We'll have you in a suit and out on the beach by morning."

Shanda couldn't help but laugh at his exuberance. He was charming, determined, and persuasive. There were many other things she admired about him, but she would not allow herself to think about them. He was going to be difficult enough to forget as it was.

The shopping center wasn't far away, and Shanda giggled at York's comments as he drove there.

"Wait until you see the suit I select for you," he joked. "It'll cover you from your neck to your knees."

The picture she imagined amused her, but she was unprepared for York's preference when she tried suits on in the store.

"That one," he said, appraising her critically with a designer's eye. He moved closer and drew her to him so that no one else could hear. "You really are the most stunning woman I've ever seen. If we don't pay for that and get out of here quickly, I'm going to take you into the fitting room and make love to you."

Her face bright with color, she looked back in the three-way mirror. The jade-colored French-cut suit rose daringly high, almost to her hipbones, making her long legs look even longer. It was belted at the waist to emphasize her curves. Surprisingly, it had a high and modest neckline, but when she glanced over her shoulder and saw how far it plunged down her back, she could only shake her head.

"We'll take it," York said, looking briefly at the clerk before his eyes met hers again.

With a long-ingrained flash of independence, Shanda shook her head. "No, we'll take the red one," she said, referring to a more modest model.

"If that's the one you want," York said easily. He motioned to the clerk. "Wrap it up. I'll pay for it while she gets dressed."

Shanda was surprised that he hadn't remained firm about his preference, and she shook her head a second time. "I've changed my mind. I'll take this one after all. And I'll pay for it myself."

York chuckled slightly. "Fine," he said, watching her with glowing eyes. He never knew what to expect from her, but he knew not to fight her. Her private space was very important to her, and he wanted her to realize that he was no threat. He wanted her to do exactly as she pleased. Just as long as he was a part of what pleased her.

It wasn't until they were on the way to Shanda's apartment to collect some of her belongings, that she realized York had his way after all. She had purchased the suit he'd wanted her to have.

"Aye, aye, aye," she muttered beneath her breath. First the chains, now the suit. She would have to proceed very cautiously with this man, very cautiously indeed.

"Pardon me?" York said.

She looked at him, then glanced away with a careless shrug. "I was only talking to myself."

York grinned. "I'd much rather you talk to me."

Shanda nodded, but fell silent. She had already said and done too much with this man. She would keep to her own counsel.

By midnight Shanda and York were sitting out on the deck of a lovely beach house perched high above the Pacific Ocean. The night was warm, and the moon was shining down on them.

Shanda found the fashion designer especially captivating in the black bathing suit he wore. He had pulled on a casual shirt, but it was left unbuttoned, and she could see the thick covering of hair on his chest in the moonlight.

"Let's take a quick dip in the ocean and call it a night," he suggested.

Shanda opened her eyes wide. "The water will be cold."

"We'll have each other to keep us warm," York said with a smile. "This section of the beach is very private."

Shanda looked away from the grin on his handsome face, but she felt an anticipatory thrill as he took a blanket in hand and led her down the long row of winding steps to the sandy beach made golden by the moon.

In the small secluded cove, the water lapped gently against the rocks near the shore, and Shanda marveled at the night beauty around her.

"Help me," York said, and Shanda turned back to find him spreading out the blanket.

When she had assisted him, he laughingly pulled her down on the softness of the sandy blanket bed.

"I really shouldn't be here," she murmured.

"Yes, you should," York whispered. "I want you here." He drew her to him and intimately entangled his legs with hers.

Shanda gloried in the feel of his muscled body against her. Wrapping her arms around him, she drew him closer.

His mouth sought hers to claim it eagerly. As his hands moved over her curves, he murmured against her lips, "Let's get rid of these barriers."

The thought startled Shanda, but as York untied the ribbon that held her suit and began to slowly slip it down her body, she arched her hips to help him. Then she watched as he stripped off his clothes.

When he lowered his body to hers, she heard his deep groan of satisfaction. "That's much better, don't

159

you think?" he asked in a passion-filled voice. "Barriers only complicate things."

"Much better," she agreed, loving the feel of him. She snuggled down into the softness of the blanket as York began to move provocatively against her, and she forgot that she was on a beach in California. She forgot that she was afraid of giving this man her love.

She only knew how she felt in his arms and how she thrilled to his touch. She heard the gentle lapping of the water at their feet, and she lost herself completely in his arms.

Shanda and York spent two days in Laguna Beach, frequenting the numerous arts and crafts shops, eating in quaint cafés and plush seafood restaurants, strolling hand-in-hand down the streets of the city like any other lovers.

She couldn't remember when she had felt so relaxed, or so fulfilled. York had been right, she told herself. She had needed the break from the tension-filled days. She had also needed the time with him before they parted forever.

She had promised herself to share the days with York one by one, as she had lived the days all of her life. After all, it was the Gypsy way. But it was becoming more difficult with York. She had begun to try to peek at the future, and no one could do that. It only caused undue anxiety.

By the third day she knew that the sweet idyll must end. They couldn't stay here forever. The thought made her sad, further reinforcing the fact that she must go. After all, she had her dancing, and he had a show to give. She didn't admit, even to herself, that there were other reasons for her to move on. Their destinies lay in different directions; there was no point in pretending otherwise.

She and York were sitting on the beach late on their third night, when she decided she could no longer put off the parting.

York had built a campfire, and when he drew her to him, he joked, "Look at the two of us here, just like a pair of Gypsies."

Oh, that it were true, Shanda thought. She spread her fingers out against the blanket and clutched at the sand beneath. "It's time for the real Gypsy to move on," she murmured, dragging each word to her lips.

York looked at her in surprise, as though he had never anticipated her leaving, and Shanda felt a shaft of pain shoot through her heart.

"You can't mean that," he insisted.

He reached out for her, and she drew away. She couldn't let him tempt her further. It was long past time to move on.

"I do mean it," she said. "You must live your life, and I must live mine."

"Come back to New York with me," he said earnestly.

"Why?" she asked. What did he want of her? What did he expect from her? Surely he knew how impossible it was for her to live in his world.

"Because I want you with me."

The words caused her heart to contract painfully. She realized that she had longed desperately to hear them, but they were only more chains to bind her tightly to him.

161

She firmly shook her head, before she could indulge in the sweet luxury of believing that they could have a future.

"I can't."

"Why?"

She looked away, not knowing how to explain. "Your world is not mine. What would I do? What would become of a wandering Gypsy dancer?" She didn't need an answer from him. Before he could say anything, she continued.

"We have enjoyed each other. That's all, and it's rare enough. Don't spoil it with anger and regret. Treasure the memory, as I will, but admit it was only a moment in time—too fleeting to capture, too fragile to last without shattering. It's the Gypsy way."

York didn't know what to say, what to think. He couldn't believe that she could just walk away. He stared at the campfire, watching the dancing flames as they ate at the slender logs, sending swirls of smoke toward the sky. He had to think of some way to convince Shanda that this wasn't a casual affair, that they had something very real and rare.

But when he turned back to speak to her, she had vanished. Angrily he faced the fire and stirred the logs, watching as fresh puffs of smoke disappeared into the air, much like his plans. He had been sure that Shanda was beginning to see how she would fit into his world, but evidently she wasn't ready yet.

There was no point in pursuing her. After all, he couldn't chain her to him. He would have to bide his time a bit longer. He trusted his instincts fully enough to believe that she cared deeply for him. But that didn't stop the ache that rose inside him at the thought of her leaving.

CHAPTER THIRTEEN

Shanda restlessly paced the colorful room she called home. She had left York over a week ago, but she couldn't cast him from her mind. She had been sure that she could forget him in her work, but his memory haunted her.

Every time she tried to concentrate on her dance steps, York's image surged into her mind. The three days with him had been too fulfilling; she had created too many memories. She could still recall in vivid detail the touch of his fingers on her skin, the way her body had thrilled to his. At last she understood that she would never be free of him until she had worked herself free.

With fierce determination she began to dance, letting his memory work for her, instead of against her. And soon she was creating inspired steps, magical leaps, and an exquisite dance.

She jumped when she heard a knock on her door. No one except York knew she was in California, so she could not still the beating of her pulse as she went to answer.

When she opened the door, she stared wide-eyed at the visitor before her. For a moment she couldn't believe her eyes. The tall, red-haired woman held a tissue in her hands and she was nervously wrapping it around and around her index finger.

"Mother?" Shanda asked, tentatively testing the word with her tongue. She was not sure she could trust her voice.

"Shanda," Kaye Wilson whispered. Suddenly her green eyes overflowed with tears, and she rushed forward to be embraced by her daughter.

"Oh, Shanda, I thought I'd never see you again. Your father forbade it. The tribe moved on—I didn't know where to look—" Her voice became lost in soft sobs.

Shanda held her tightly, crooning a Gypsy term of endearment. Then she guided Kaye into the room and held her at arms' length so that she could look at her.

"I couldn't find you either," she murmured. "I wanted so much to see you again, but you were just gone."

"You looked for me?" Kaye asked, her eyes intense. "I was so afraid that you would hate me for leaving you behind."

Shanda shook her head as she took her mother by the hand and led her to the couch. "How could I ever hate you?" she asked. "I missed you and I loved you, but I could only think that you had gained your freedom at last."

Kaye looked away. "I wasn't a good Gypsy wife,

Shanda, and I didn't live by the tribe's code. But believe me when I say that I never wanted my freedom from your father. I loved him." She glanced down at her hands. "I wasn't able to bend to his wishes, but I want you to know that I loved him very much."

"But he hurt you so many times," Shanda said, the memory of those times rising fresh in her mind.

"His behavior was based on his heritage. I didn't understand his world."

The words caused Shanda to think of York, and she didn't want to do that. She missed him too much.

"I searched for you wherever my travels took me," she told her mother, "but there were too many Kaye Wilsons and too many dead ends." She laughed nervously. "I suspected that you were using your maiden name, but I looked under both Wilson and Nicholas to no avail."

Kaye seemed embarrassed. "I married again, Shanda," she confessed. "My name is Swenson."

"You married again?" Shanda repeated. She had been sure that her mother had learned her lesson with her Gypsy husband.

Kaye brushed at her tears. "Yes—three years ago," she said, her face turning pink. "Oh, Shanda, it's wonderful this time."

"But once you were free, why did you remarry?" Shanda asked, her voice full of confusion. "You were your own woman at last."

Kaye smiled a sweet and dreamy smile. "Love *is* freedom, Shanda. I fell in love again. When it happens, you'll realize that the right man is worth what you're calling your freedom."

Shanda didn't believe that. She could never believe that.

"Love isn't binding," Kaye added softly. "It's a gift beyond words. In spite of all the pain it sometimes brings, it also brings great joy. But surely you do know that already. Aren't you in love with that charming man who contacted me?"

"Who?" Shanda asked, the echo of her heartbeats sounding wildly in her ears.

"Why, York. York Summerfield."

"York?" Shanda whispered.

Kaye nodded. "He said he found me through a private detective, and he told me where you were."

Shanda smiled. York and his detective who apparently had the nose of a bloodhound.

"Are you in love with him?" Kaye repeated.

Her mother's question reverberated through Shanda's mind. Suddenly, she knew precisely what price she had paid for the gold chains York Summerfield had given her: She had paid with her heart.

Despite all her warnings and precautions, she *was* in love with the *gajó* stranger. She didn't know how or why or when. She only knew as a woman does, that she was in love with him.

Struck dumb by the revelation, she could only nod her head.

"Do you plan to marry him?"

Shanda looked at her mother in alarm. "No!" she said fiercely.

"But why?" Kaye asked. "If you love him and he loves you, why not marry?"

Looking away, Shanda traced the thin line of gold around her neck. York hadn't asked her to marry him. He had never even said he loved her. And even if he had, love wasn't enough.

"It would never work," Shanda murmured. "Look what happened between you and my father. It would be the same thing with York and me. Our worlds are too different. He wants to chain me, to tie me down, and I couldn't exist like that."

"Shanda, please don't make the mistake of basing your life on someone else's mistakes. What happened between your father and me has nothing to do with you and your young man. I'm sure he loves you very much. He went to great trouble to find me. He told me that he wants to help you rebuild your past, and I admire any man who is that sensitive."

Shanda locked her fingers in the chains around her neck. York *had* done an amazingly sensitive thing by finding her mother for her. She wouldn't forget it. But it hurt too much to think about York right now.

"Enough about me," she said brightly. "I want to hear all about you."

The night of York's show, he was backstage in the middle of what seemed to be a madhouse. Beautiful women hustled around furiously, laughing and shouting at each other as they pulled off one dress and pulled on another.

Amid racks of clothes, everyone seemed to be in a constant state of undress. York stood in the midst of some of the most gorgeous models in the world, but he hardly noticed that they were in skimpy bras and panties and half-slips.

Usually he would be joking with them, trying to ease some of the tension of the quick clothes changes, but tonight he couldn't seem to get in the spirit of the event. His lovely white dress hung on a rack, waiting for the model who had finally been chosen to slip it on, and York could only think how badly he had wanted Shanda to model it.

Once he had visualized the dress on her, he couldn't see it on anyone else. He had told Shanda the date and the place of his show, and she knew where he lived. Right up to the opening of the show he had hoped that she would turn up. Clearly it had been a foolish hope, but he could not hide his disappointment.

As if fervent wishing had produced her, Shanda suddenly appeared in the room. There was a low hum of excitement as people began to question her unexpected presence, and York looked around to see what the additional commotion was all about. For a minute he was sure that the Gypsy was a figment of his imagination.

But Shanda Nicholas was all too real. She had slipped backstage undetected, and she had lingered by the door, watching all the pandemonium. She had also watched York.

She had told herself that she had simply been too curious to stay away. The show might prove interesting. She also told herself that she was here because of her gratitude to York for finding her mother. But in the back of her mind she knew the real reason: she was here because she was in love with York and he had asked her to model.

York didn't look away from her as he approached Shanda. He was too afraid she would vanish before his very eyes. He was astonished to see her. There, in the midst of all the hurly-burly, she stood out like a bright star, all fire and life and energy.

"Shanda," he said with incredible restraint, "when did you get back in town?"

"Two days ago."

He wanted to ask why she hadn't contacted him, but he held his tongue. "Where are you staying?"

"My old apartment was still vacant, so I took it."

There was an awkward pause while they looked at each other. The chaos continued all around them, but he didn't even notice it.

"I'm glad you decided to come," he said, assuming the same casual attitude Shanda had.

She gave him a careless shrug. She didn't want him to know all the reasons she had come. "I wanted to see what it was all about. I'll model the dress if you still want me to."

York tried not to show his excitement. He had bided his time, and Shanda had come to him. He wasn't fool enough to think she was making any kind of commitment, but she had taken a step into his world. He viewed it as a good sign.

"Fine. I'd like that." He motioned to a thin woman. "Please take Shanda to makeup. She'll be wearing the final number, the white dress."

The woman's expression didn't betray her surprise as she led Shanda over to a vanity with a lighted mirror. York watched for a moment, then he left the room. He wanted to see Shanda in the dress right along with the rest of the audience. He wanted to feel their response to his Gypsy beauty.

Despite her outward calm, Shanda was a nervous wreck as she sat in front of the makeup mirror. She had watched some of the show, but she was no model. She was very eager to do justice to York's dress, but she wasn't sure what was expected of her. While she was being coiffured and groomed, she listened to the accolades being heaped upon York for his new line, and she grew even more tense.

As she watched the high-strung artist paint her face with enchanting colors, Shanda heard a cry of recognition behind her. When she looked in the mirror, she saw a reflection of the blonde York had been with the first night she met him. To her surprise, the woman was pointing at her and gesturing madly.

"How do we look?" the makeup artist asked, leaning over her proudly.

"Fine," Shanda murmured distractedly, and in truth she had never found herself more attractive. "Thank you."

She slipped out of the makeup chair and went into the dressing room, but not before she heard Hellyn Anderson's low, clear voice. "I honestly can't believe it. York bet me a thousand dollars that he could get the Gypsy to model, and there she is in the flesh. That vagrant dancer has cost me a thousand dollars!"

The model Hellyn was talking to squealed in delight. "No kidding! I wondered why on earth she was here. York did it on a bet! My God, but that's wild! Only he would do something like that."

"Come, dearie," the thin woman said, motioning to Shanda. She held out the white dress Shanda was to model, and for a moment the image of woman and dress blurred before Shanda's eyes.

York had wanted her to model his dress as a lark! He had made a *bet* with the blonde for a thousand dollars! The muscles tightened in her stomach, and she thought she might be ill as she recalled how he had sat with the blonde and laughed the first night he watched her dance.

He had been laughing at her. He had made a bigger fool of her than she had ever imagined. Not only had he stolen her heart and taken her soul, he had made her a laughingstock in his world. She had traded her pride and her body for his jewelry and his jest and his deceitful gestures. She had been only a vagrant Gypsy dancer. Now she was his Gypsy joke.

Her eyes glittered and her lips tightened into a thin line. For just a moment she thought of ripping his pretty white dress to shreds and flinging it in his face.

Her thoughts spun wildly. York Summerfield would not get the best of her! She *would* model his dress, but she would do it her way! She would leave an impression that he would never forget!

Her head held high, she loosened her long ebony hair from the elegant hairdo she had been given. When it fell free around her shoulders, she tossed it back defiantly.

"You shouldn't have done that!" the woman attending her exclaimed in alarm, but Shanda ignored her.

The baffled woman didn't seem to know what to do. While she looked around, trying to decide, Shanda finished her own dressing.

Paying no attention to the frowning woman, she stared at the stunning white dress, quickly assessing its possibilities. A sleek, silky confection, it had a lacy handkerchief-effect hem and two long, wide, matching pieces of lace that crisscrossed her bosom to tie at the back of her waist.

When the woman nervously tried to tie them, Shanda brushed her hands aside. "But this is the way to wear the dress," the woman moaned.

"I'll wear it as I see fit," Shanda said firmly, turning away.

"Wait!" the flustered woman cried. "The shoes!"

With a defiant shake of her head, Shanda spurned the exquisite white heels.

"I don't want them."

The music that signaled her entrance began, and ignoring the woman's pleas to finish dressing, Shanda marched toward the runway.

Everyone was waiting for the pièce de résistance, and she intended to give it to them. She could feel the tension in the audience, and she heard the excitement backstage as word spread that she wasn't properly dressed in York's masterpiece. York had conveniently provided her with music with a Gypsy beat, and Shanda decided to do what she did best.

She looked back over her shoulder just in time to see several people heading in her direction, whispering heatedly and gesturing madly.

"Stop her!" someone said.

Her dark eyes flashing rebelliously, Shanda let her gaze rake over her pursuers. "*Gajé* fools!" she muttered contemptuously, then she slipped up to the curtain.

Holding one of the lace ties in front of her face like a veil, she plunged out on stage in one fantastic leap before anyone backstage could catch her.

The stuffy, sophisticated audience gasped as one at

the startling and unexpected move. They had been eagerly and patiently expecting another in the long line of stately, elegant models who strolled out at leisure and paraded and postured.

Shanda had never seen so many people momentarily lose their composure in her life. Her bare feet slapping the floor, she twirled and spun in York's exquisite white dress, hiking it up to her thighs and flashing it around her body like a cape.

Clearly the audience had never seen anything like it, and flashbulbs began to go off like firecrackers as fashion news hounds recorded the moment for their papers. Shanda found the rapid beat and the challenge of the moment so heady that she danced as never before, daring the fashion aficionados to look away from her fantastic display of York's top number from his collection.

The song was much too brief for her satisfaction, but when the music ended, she strutted and postured in an exaggerated mockery of the other models. Then she calmly made her way backstage as though she had merely performed as the others had.

For a long, tense moment, there was total silence. Then abruptly, the silence was shattered by fierce clapping.

In the madness of the moment, Shanda quickly slipped into the dressing room and changed clothes, flinging the beautiful white dress to the floor. Then, while everyone surrounded York, congratulating him on pulling off such an unprecedented show, Shanda slipped out a back way.

173

York had been sitting out in the audience to get the full effect of his dress on his lovely Gypsy lady. Right along with the rest of the viewers, he had been astounded to see Shanda plunge onto the stage, and along with the others, he had sat breathlessly through her performance. And it *was* a performance.

But he had been both amused and delighted by it, even before the others broke into applause. He had wanted Shanda's freshness, her vitality, her spirit in his show. True, he hadn't expected her to dance, but he had enjoyed it immensely. Shanda had given the dress personality, versatility, beauty.

He was eager to congratulate her, but he couldn't make his way through the people to her. Although impatient, he tried to be gracious and deserving of the compliments and accolades heaped upon him as he worked his way backstage. He could hardly wait to tell Shanda what a hit she had been!

In her small apartment Shanda ripped the necklace York had given her from around her neck and flung it on the floor. "Baa!" she cried bitterly. "No one makes a fool of Shanda Nicholas!"

The beautiful thin chains spilled across the floor, and Shanda went over and trampled them for good measure. She had learned her lesson. No one would succeed in chaining her again, and no one would again trick her into falling in love. Especially no pretty *gajó* fool who thought he owned the world.

Reaching up, she took the earrings from her ears and slung them across the room, not caring where they landed. Next came the ankle bracelet. Jerking it from her leg, she threw it against a nearby wall. She hadn't worn the belt, but now she sought it out in her possessions. When she found it, it met the same fate as the other jewelry.

Then she picked up her bags and stormed out of the apartment. She never wanted to see this place or York Summerfield again. She hoped his show was a total disaster and that she had been the one to make it so.

But she took no pleasure in her anger as she strode to the nearest subway. She had already given York the most important part of herself. She could throw off hundreds of chains and she still wouldn't be free. She was bound to him by her love just as surely as if he had handcuffed her. He had trapped the Gypsy in her, and she didn't know how she would ever be free.

York was high with the feeling of success as he finally managed to get backstage. He wanted nothing more in the entire world than to swing his Gypsy beauty up in his arms and run out into the night with her. He didn't care if she never modeled another dress. She had stepped into his world and conquered it.

"Where is she?" he asked as he made his way through the models and agency heads and other members of the fashion world who were laughing and gossiping as they lingered, waiting for him to announce where the traditional celebration party would be held.

He hadn't planned anything, but he would stage something impromptu. He and Shanda would put in a token appearance, then vanish. Tonight he wanted her strictly to himself. Unless, of course, she wanted to share her triumph with the others.

"Where is who?" someone asked, most of the attention focused on the designer now.

York grinned. "Who? Who else? My Gypsy lady."

He caught a flicker of jealousy, but he didn't have time to indulge it. "Where is she?"

There were choruses of "I don't know," and he tried not to show his impatience as he made his way to the dressing room.

The thin lady was anxiously smoothing out the wrinkles on the white dress Shanda had tossed to the floor.

"Where is she?" York demanded, tension beginning to tighten his chest muscles.

The woman looked at him in alarm. "She's gone."

"Gone?"

"She took off the dress, threw it on the floor, and left."

York told himself to remain calm, but he didn't know if it was possible. He was furious this time. He was tired of Shanda dancing into his life, stirring it up, and vanishing. He had been patient, he had played the game, and now it was time for a long overdue confrontation.

People were calling his name, but he couldn't hear a word they said until Hellyn caught up with him and grasped his arm. "York, for pity's sake, where are you going?"

"Shanda's gone," he muttered distractedly. "I'm going to find her."

Hellyn laughed. "What does it matter now? You proved your point, didn't you? You got her to model

—if that's what you want to call it. I can't believe you did it. Even more, I can't believe I owe you a thousand dollars!"

"What?" he asked crossly. He didn't have time to waste.

"The bet. Now don't tell me you forgot that you bet me a thousand dollars you could get the Gypsy to model. Why didn't I keep my big mouth shut?"

For a moment York still didn't know what she was talking about. Then it dawned on him. Yes, *the bet!* He had made a wager with her that first night, before he became involved with Shanda. He had completely forgotten about it, so enchanted was he with the Gypsy dancer.

"Did you say something to Shanda about the bet?" he demanded, his fingers tightening on her shoulders.

Hellyn shook her head. "No, and you don't need to be so angry. You won."

York's handsome features twisted unhappily. "Did you tell someone else about it tonight?"

Hellyn shrugged. "Yes, some of the models. I couldn't believe my eyes when I saw the girl, and I mentioned the bet to a couple of them."

"Oh, God," York groaned miserably. "She must have heard you."

"York, will you tell me what's going on?" Hellyn said in exasperated tones. "You don't sound very happy about winning."

He shook his head. "I'm sorry, Hellyn, but I think I've just lost the most important thing in my life." He startled himself with the admission, but he knew that it was all too true. "Give your thousand dollars to charity," he said. "I don't want it." He brushed past her. "Excuse me. I've got to leave."

He raced out to his car. When he pulled open the door, the startled chauffeur almost tumbled out.

"Excuse me, sir. I didn't see you," he apologized.

York crammed some money in his hand. "Take a cab home. I won't be needing you tonight." Then he slid into the car and roared off into the dark night.

His hands were trembling when he walked up to Shanda's apartment and rapped on the door. When no one answered, he pounded harder and called her name. He still got no response. In vain he tried to peek into the windows, but all the shades were closed.

Desperate, he knocked at the next-door apartment, where he knew Vagan and Miguel had lived. When a fierce-looking dark man answered, York announced, "I think Shanda's ill next door. Do you have a key?"

The bearded man looked at him suspiciously, then walked away. A moment later he came back with two long-haired women. Without a word the three of them preceded him to Shanda's apartment, where one of the women unlocked the door.

When the man had turned on a light, they all stepped inside, filling up the doorway so that York couldn't enter. "Shanda!" the man bellowed. Then he called out something in Romany.

When Shanda didn't appear, he stepped farther into the house, the women behind him. York was able to peer over their shoulders, and he saw that there was no point in lingering. He had his answers.

The jewelry he had given the Gypsy lay in broken,

crumpled heaps about the big room. But otherwise there was no sign that Shanda had lived in the New York apartment. The room was empty of all her possessions.

His heart beating wildly, York turned on his heel and headed back to the car. He had to find his Gypsy lady. He didn't know where or how. But he knew that he had to find her.

CHAPTER FOURTEEN

York searched frantically for Shanda, but it was as though she had vanished from the face of the earth. Charley immediately followed up on the latest information—Shanda's mother, the last club where Fever had played the night the group broke up, the apartment Shanda had occupied in California, the area where Vagan and Miguel had lived. But there was nothing. Not a trace of her.

As York listened to Charley's report on the phone, his heart sank. "She has to be somewhere," he insisted. "Dig harder. I'll pay whatever it's worth to you."

Charley sighed tiredly on the other end of the line. "It's not the money, York," he said. "I really can't find the girl. You don't know these Gypsies. They're always on the move. They use duplicate names. They live with relatives. They're the hidden Americans."

"But Shanda has to make a living," York insisted

rationally. "Check all the clubs anywhere who hire exotic dancers."

Again Charley sighed. "She could lay low for weeks without working, York, and when she does work, she books under the group name. You yourself said her group disbanded. She could be performing with anyone anywhere. I can't find her."

York's fingers tightened on the phone and he resisted the urge to slam it down in frustration. "Keep looking, Charley," he said firmly. "You're the best I can get. You're my only hope."

"It's your money," the other man said with resignation. "But it's like beating a dead horse, I'm telling you."

When York had replaced the phone in its cradle, he leaned forward in his chair and rested his elbows on his desk. Why? he kept asking himself. Why? Why had she gone? Why hadn't she at least talked to him? If she'd overheard Hellyn, had she believed that a bet was all there was to their relationship? It was the only explanation.

He didn't understand how Shanda could have lain in his arms, how she could have felt his heart beat against hers, felt the love he had for her, and thought that he had wanted her only to win a thousand-dollar bet. He simply couldn't believe that was true. There had to be more to it than that. He couldn't help but believe it.

His gaze was drawn to the pages of the fashion magazines that now flaunted the Gypsy beauty's picture. In a sudden burst of anger he raked all the magazines off his desk, knocking them to the floor.

"Damn you, Shanda," he groaned helplessly.

"Damn you for coming into my life, and damn you for not caring enough to stay!"

Restlessly Shanda paced the isolated picnic grounds where several Gypsy tribes had gathered for fun and feasting. There was music and dancing and frivolity, but she couldn't get into the spirit of it. Her heart was heavy. She still wore York's chains just as surely as if she had never torn them from her body, and she didn't know how to be free of his shackles of love.

She seemed to have no world of her own now, neither Gypsy or *gajé*. She didn't feel at home anywhere, and all she could think of was York's arms around her.

"Come and dance, Shanda!" a huge man called out. "We all want to see your skill."

Trying to force a smile, Shanda shook her head. "Later." She gestured to her stomach. "I ate too much food. I would roll like a watermelon."

Everyone laughed, and Shanda smiled, glad to be free of the burden of performing for the group. She frowned at her own thoughts. She had never considered dancing for her people a burden. All Gypsies danced.

She shook her head. She had only known York several weeks, and already she was thinking like the *gajé*. Turning away, she headed down the hill to the river. Maybe she could let the water wash away her troubles, but she doubted it. She didn't think an ocean could cure what ailed her. Only York could, and she didn't want to see him again as long as she lived.

"York, you *prikáza,*" she whispered brokenly, tears coming to her eyes. A vision of his handsome face appeared before her, and though it was broken and blurred by the tears that tumbled down her cheeks, she could not wash it away.

Finding a secluded spot on the riverbank, she sat down, rested her arms on her legs, and began to weep.

One week slipped into two, and two into three. Shanda couldn't stay idle any longer. She thought she would go crazy with the memories of York Summerfield. The only way she could hope to get him out of her blood was by dancing until she was too weary to think about him. But although she had discussed getting a new group together, she had found no one in her travels that she wanted to dance with.

Miguel and Vagan were her partners and she longed to work with them again. Before the month ended, she traced Miguel to a Gypsy habitat in upper New York State. Without a word she turned up at the house he shared with several other Gypsies.

"Shanda, come in!" he cried excitedly. "I've been looking for you."

She seemed puzzled. The Gypsy grapevine was extremely efficient. Families were always notifying one another that a particular person was searching for them, and despite all the traveling, it was easy enough to seek out a Gypsy by word of mouth.

"You've been on the move constantly for weeks," Miguel stressed. "Everyone I contacted said you had just moved on."

Shanda smiled a little sadly. She herself hadn't realized how restless she had been. "I'm sorry," she said. "I can't seem to settle in. I need to work. Have you found another violinist?"

Miguel shook his head. "Not another one, but how would you feel about dancing with Vagan and me again?"

Before Shanda could reply, Miguel added, "He's taken a Gypsy wife, Shanda. I think you'll find him changed, and certainly no longer trying to rule you." He laughed. "Vagan's in love with a woman who loves him, and she's an obedient Gypsy wife. He's quite happy."

Shanda cringed at the notion of a woman being an *obedient* wife—Gypsy or *gajé*—but she was pleased for Vagan.

"In that case I'd be delighted to dance with you two again." She laughed softly. "Vagan in love. I thought I'd never see it, but I'm thrilled. You know, Miguel, he is the best violinist I know."

Miguel nodded. "We want to open across the border in Canada. Vagan's already found a spot."

"Then he knew you would be contacting me?"

"Yes, of course. You're the best Gypsy dancer who ever lived. Vagan respects your talent. He just didn't know how you would feel after he fought with your man."

Shanda felt herself withdrawing at the mention of York. Love had treated her too unkindly. She didn't want to talk about "her man."

"How is he?" Miguel asked before she could change the subject.

"Who?"

Miguel laughed. "So that's how it is? You found that you didn't like modeling for the *gajé*, did you?"

Shanda laughed mockingly. "Modeling? Did I model?"

Miguel caught the bitterness in her laugh and was sensitive enough to change the subject. "When will you be ready to go to Canada?"

She gestured to her clothes and her canvas bag. "I need to make one phone call, and I'm ready to go. I'm a Gypsy, remember?"

Laughing cheerfully, Miguel nodded. "So you are. Welcome back, Shanda."

York's hunt for the Gypsy went on relentlessly, but he could not track her down. Day after day, week after week, he ignored his work to concentrate on the search. He had no desire to complete his spring line, for he couldn't look at the sketches of the Gypsy clothing without thinking of Shanda, and already he was going mad from thoughts of her.

York was desperate by the time Charley called to say that Shanda had finally contacted Kaye, and the mother thought she knew where her daughter was.

"Finally," York breathed. "Finally."

Summer was almost at an end by the time the group, with a new name—Free—booked into the exclusive club on the Canadian border. Shanda was feeling good about working again. She had new dances, new costumes, and she was determined to put the past behind her.

Vagan was content as she had never known him to be, and Shanda liked his young Gypsy bride. The girl wanted only to please, and for the first time in months there was no disharmony in the group.

Shanda was looking forward to the first performance with great anticipation. Dressed in white lace and silk, she ignored the influence York had had on her costume design as she pulled a lace shawl across her face in preparation for her first number.

The lights dimmed, the music began, and Shanda exploded onto the stage with all the energy and frustration that had been bottled up inside her for too long. She cried out Romany phrases as she danced across the floor, pouring her heart and soul into the dance. She felt exuberant! And she promised herself that she wouldn't think of York Summerfield a single time tonight.

The promise was short-lived. *"O Del!"* she agonized aloud as she looked out into her audience for the first time. Like a recurring bad dream, she imagined York's image on the man sitting right in front, center stage.

Knowing her mind had to be playing tricks this time, she continued to dance, her eyes closed so that she wouldn't see the stranger wearing York's features. But no matter how she tried, she couldn't keep from looking back at the man.

She sucked in her breath. It *was* York! It really was York! Shanda didn't know why or how he was here, but he was. Her heart pounding savagely, she tried to fashion some plan of escape when her performance was over, but by the time the show had ended, she was frantic.

If Vagan or Miguel had seen the fashion designer, neither let on. Shanda danced her final number, then left the stage. She was desperate by the time she returned to her dressing room. Vagan's wife was waiting to help her change her costume, but she excused her. She didn't want the younger woman to witness the scene with York, and she was sure there would be one. York would seek her out, otherwise why would he be here?

Suddenly she stopped and drew in a steadying breath. Why was she running again? Why was she trying to escape York Summerfield? She would give him the piece of her mind that he deserved and never see his face again! She would tell him what she thought of him and his bet!

She heard his steps in the hall. There was a brief pause when York encountered Vagan and Miguel, and to Shanda's ire, she heard Vagan tell the designer that they had no quarrel with him.

Her face flaming, Shanda spun around to confront York as he boldly opened the door to her dressing room. Her heart began to beat erratically. She had always found it difficult to stand so near him, but she drew on her anger and pain now.

"How did you find me, and why have you tracked me down?" she demanded with a haughty tilt of her chin.

"I called your mother," he said sharply. "At least you had enough decency to tell *her* where you'd gone."

"My mother had no right to tell you where I was," she exclaimed.

"She did it because she understands you better than you do yourself," York said. "Damn you, Shanda, why did you run out on me?"

187

With as little warning to herself as to York, Shanda strode across the room and slapped him across the face. "You know why! I hope the dress I modeled never sold a single copy!" she cried.

She drew back her hand to strike him again, but York grasped it in his. When Shanda raised the other hand, he caught that one too.

"You damned, enchanting witch, stop fighting and running, and talk to me! If you're referring to the bet I made with Hellyn, say so."

He twisted her arms behind her back and dragged her against him until her body touched his and her lips were inches away. "But before you tell me you reacted to something you overheard without even confronting me, I'll tell you yes, I did make a thousand-dollar bet that I could get you to model."

His breath was warm on her face, and his eyes were glowing in that hypnotic way. "But that was before I knew you." He lowered his head ever so slightly and his lips lightly caressed hers. "It was before I had kissed you." He freed her hands and drew her more fiercely against him. "It was before I had touched you, held you, known the wonder and magic of you."

He saw that her eyes were closed against him, and her head was turned aside. "Let me go," she demanded. "I hate you. You made a fool of me. You made me your Gypsy joke."

"I would never do that," he said thickly. "I asked you to model because I knew you could do for my dress what no other woman could."

He tilted her chin until she was forced to look at him. "And I'm sorry to tell you, but I've never sold so

188

many copies of one dress in my life. I loved your dance, and the audience and media did too. You were the hit of the show, Gypsy beauty. You did what I thought you could do."

Shanda twisted her head away from him. Sensing her withdrawal, York whispered, "I'm sorry if I hurt you, Shanda. That was never my intention, I promise you. I was always sincere with you. I wanted you only for yourself. I knew that my world would be difficult for you, and I tried to give you time to adjust, but you were determined to shut me out, to keep up your barriers."

When Shanda still didn't speak, he sighed raggedly. Maybe he had been the fool. He couldn't cage a dream; he couldn't catch the wind; he couldn't make the Gypsy want him.

"If you really don't want me in your life—" He made himself continue. ". . . tell me so now, and I'll go away and leave you alone."

Shanda could feel the tears sting the backs of her eyes. How could she tell the man she loved that she didn't want him? How could she send him away again? He had looked into her eyes once more, touched her, reached out and held her heart and soul in his hands.

When she didn't speak, York felt as if he had been left all alone on a desert island. He had read her wrong. He had cared so much for her that he had told himself she cared equally for him. Hellyn's words came to haunt him a third time. He *was* too spoiled. He had thought that Shanda would want to be in his world, just because he had wanted her to be there.

His hands fell to his sides. He allowed himself the

painful luxury of studying her gorgeous features—
her long, dark lashes covering her closed eyes, her
beautiful nose and mouth, her luxuriant black hair,
her exquisite body. Then he silently turned away.

He had almost reached the door when she called
his name. "York!"

He whirled around and she held herself rigidly
before him.

"I can't fight you any longer!" she cried bitterly. "I
can't let you go. I'll wear your chains, if I must. Right
or wrong, *gajó* or not, you're my destiny."

Puzzled, York stared at her. "What are you saying?
What chains?"

Her eyes green and pained, she looked up at him.
"I'm a Gypsy in my soul, York. That's what I am and
what I want to be. Your world is not mine. I want to
live my own life. I don't want a man telling me what
to do and when to do it. I don't want to model."

She drew in a harsh breath. "I knew your inten-
tions when you gave me the first gift—the belt of
chains to show you meant to rule me, to control me.
But I fell in love with you anyway."

Sheer relief softened the haggard lines of York's
face. His smile was tender and his eyes were earnest
as he shook his head in wonder. At last he understood
why she had fought so hard and run so far.

"Shanda, please listen to me. I love you too. I want
nothing but your love in return. I would never, never
restrain your free spirit. It's part of you that I love.
My designs are only on your heart. I didn't give you
chains to bind you, and I don't care if you never
model another dress as long as you live."

He realized that he meant that with all his heart.

He had based his spring line on her, but it meant nothing if he lost her. "You are free to live your own life, to dance, to travel, to be with your people—or mine. I only ask that I be some part of your life."

"But we live in two different worlds," she whispered, unable to believe what she was hearing.

He shook his head. "No, Shanda. There is only one world—ours. I'm not asking you to give up anything for me. I'd like to marry you. I'd like to be the father of your children. But most of all, I only want to love you."

Her mother's words about love being freedom echoed in Shanda's mind, and she realized her mother was right.

Her eyes glowed as they met York's, and at last she gave her heart permission to love the *gajó* stranger who was willing to let her be as free as she wanted to be.

She tossed back her ebony hair. "I might want to model again," she said. "I might model your Gypsy line. I *was* good, wasn't I?"

"Very good," he agreed with a smile. "Very, very good."

Then he drew her to him and dipped his head to claim her mouth.

Shanda went into his arms and eagerly met the fire in his kiss. She had finally found her world in York's heart.

Now you can reserve May's Candlelights *before* they're published!

💜 You'll have copies set aside for *you* the instant they come off press.

💜 You'll save yourself precious shopping time by arranging for *home delivery.*

💜 You'll feel proud and efficient about organizing a system that *guarantees* delivery.

💜 You'll avoid the disappointment of not finding *every* title you want and need.

ECSTASY SUPREMES $2.75 each

- ☐ 121 **BEYOND A DOUBT,** Eleanor Woods 10655-9-24
- ☐ 122 **TORCH SONG,** Lee Magner 18718-4-22
- ☐ 123 **CUPID'S DILEMMA,** Ginger Chambers . . 11632-5-46
- ☐ 124 **A FRAGILE DECEPTION,** Jane Atkin 12695-9-30

ECSTASY ROMANCES $2.25 each

- ☐ 426 **FANTASY LOVER,** Anne Silverlock 12438-7-73
- ☐ 427 **PLAYING WITH FIRE,** Donna Kimel Vitek . 16983-6-81
- ☐ 428 **JUST A LOT MORE TO LOVE,** Lynn Patrick 14409-4-25
- ☐ 429 **HOT ON HIS TRAIL,** Lori Copeland 13777-2-13
- ☐ 430 **PRISONER OF PASSION,** Suzannah Davis 17110-5-28
- ☐ 431 **LOVE MAKES THE DIFFERENCE,** Emily Elliott 13774-8-32
- ☐ 432 **ROOM FOR TWO,** Joan Grove 17476-7-34
- ☐ 433 **THE BITTER WITH THE SWEET,** Alison Tyler 10583-8-21

At your local bookstore or use this handy coupon for ordering:

DELL READERS SERVICE—DEPT. B1013A
P.O. BOX 1000, PINE BROOK, N.J. 07058

Please send me the above title(s). I am enclosing $_____ (please add 75¢ per copy to cover postage and handling). Send check or money order—no cash or COODs. Please allow 3-4 weeks for shipment.
CANADIAN ORDERS: please submit in U.S. dollars.

Ms Mrs Mr _____

Address_____

City State_____ Zip _____